"All you have to do is say yes to my proposal."

Sabrina winced. Bad choice of word. "Proposition," she amended.

Jake rubbed his temples. "This is the kind of idea only you could come up with. Breaking up with you was like breaking out of Fairyland."

Her eyes smarted, but she said airily, "And I'll bet you miss the magic."

His head jerked, but he held her gaze, staring her down for several long seconds.

"You're overlooking one small fact," he said. "Namely, you're the last woman on earth I would marry."

Dear Reader,

I read my first romance novel when I was fourteen years old—I was home from school with a virus, and my mom gave me one of her Harlequin books to pass the time. It was written by Kathryn Blair, who also wrote as Rosalind Brett and Celine Conway (though it took me a while to figure out my three favorite authors were the same person!).

I loved those books! They set such high ideals for the kind of devotion a woman should expect from a man...and I have to say I carried those ideals through my teens into my dating life, and ultimately to meeting my husband. I've heard people say romance novels set "unrealistic" expectations. Well, if expecting my guy to love me to bits for the rest of his life is unrealistic, who needs realism!

For me, romance novels are about the best that love between a man and a woman can be. Finding that love is seldom easy—in *Her So-Called Fiancé*, as in all my books, the hero and heroine have to work hard. But, of course, it's worth it.

I do hope you enjoy *Her So-Called Fiancé*. To read a couple of extra After-the-End scenes, visit the For Readers page at www.abbygaines.com.

Abby Gaines

Her So-Called Fiancé
Abby Gaines

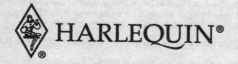

HARLEQUIN®

TORONTO • NEW YORK • LONDON
AMSTERDAM • PARIS • SYDNEY • HAMBURG
STOCKHOLM • ATHENS • TOKYO • MILAN • MADRID
PRAGUE • WARSAW • BUDAPEST • AUCKLAND

Recycling programs
for this product may
not exist in your area.

ISBN-13: 978-0-373-71585-5

HER SO-CALLED FIANCÉ

www.eHarlequin.com

Printed in U.S.A.

ABOUT THE AUTHOR

Abby Gaines wrote her first romance novel as a teenager. She typed it up and sent it to Mills & Boon in London, who promptly rejected it. A flirtation with a science fiction novel never really got off the ground, so Abby put aside her writing ambitions as she went to college, then began her working life at IBM. When she and her husband had their first baby, Abby worked from home as a freelance business journalist...and soon after that the urge to write romance resurfaced. It was another five long years before Abby sold her first novel to Harlequin Superromance in 2006. She also writes for Harlequin NASCAR.

Abby lives with her husband and children—and a labradoodle and a cat—in a house with enough stairs to keep her fit and a sun-filled office whose sea view provides inspiration for the funny, tender romances she loves to write. Visit her at www.abbygaines.com.

Books by Abby Gaines

HARLEQUIN SUPERROMANCE
1397—WHOSE LIE IS IT ANYWAY?
1414—MARRIED BY MISTAKE
1480—THE DIAPER DIARIES
1539—THE GROOM CAME BACK

HARLEQUIN NASCAR
BACK ON TRACK
FULLY ENGAGED

Don't miss any of our special offers. Write to us at the following address for information on our newest releases.

Harlequin Reader Service
U.S.: 3010 Walden Ave., P.O. Box 1325, Buffalo, NY 14269
Canadian: P.O. Box 609, Fort Erie, Ont. L2A 5X3

With love to Tessa Radley, one of the smartest, savviest and most generous women I know.

Thanks, hon!

CHAPTER ONE

SABRINA MERRITT COUNTED at least a dozen photographers waiting for her to exit the gate area at Atlanta's Hartsfield-Jackson Airport. They all had their lenses trained on her legs, which two days ago had been labeled "chunky" by beauty pageant pundits.

Great. It had been humiliating enough seeing close-ups of her thighs on national television. Now the local media, the papers read by everyone who mattered to her, were about to jump on the bandwagon.

"Sabrina, this way," one of the photographers called.

She ignored him, certain that if she so much as met anyone's eyes, the smile she'd rehearsed in her compact mirror as the plane taxied to the gate would fall off her face. Seven months as Miss Georgia had made her thick-skinned about personal criticism. But to be slammed so publicly, just when she needed people to take her seriously, and over something so meaningless to anyone but herself as her *legs*...

Glassy-eyed, she scanned the crowd, in search of her good friend Tyler, who'd said he would meet her. Darn it, he'd *promised*.

Then she saw the lone man beyond the media group. Not Tyler.

Jake Warrington.

The way he leaned his tall frame against a pillar might appear nonchalant, but the rigidity of his shoulders and the thumbs hooked in the pockets of his jeans proclaimed *I know what I want and no one's going to stop me.*

That was Jake, all right.

Was he here to gloat? Sabrina lifted her chin. She was strong and capable, even if nobody else had figured that out yet. She tapped a finger against her cheek and announced, "I'm up here, folks."

A sheepish laugh rippled through the photographers. They tilted their cameras higher—but not before they'd snapped their shots of her thighs.

Concealing her legs beneath a long, filmy sunshine-yellow sundress didn't seem to have lessened anyone's interest in them. Sabrina quashed the urge to spread her hands protectively over the delicate fabric.

She'd flown home to Atlanta a day ahead of her official schedule, in the hope of eluding the media. How stupidly naive. If Jake had been the one facing a media meltdown, he'd have anticipated this hoo-ha and prepared a speech.

"Sabrina, you're the first Miss Georgia in two decades to be eliminated from the Miss U.S.A. Pageant in the first round." A female TV reporter oozed fake sympathy.

"Good grief, is that right?" That fact, along with every other mortifying detail of her failure, had been endlessly recycled in the media over the past few days.

Presumably for the benefit of the one person in some remote corner of Alaska who hadn't yet heard about her chunky thighs.

A couple of the men caught the gleam in Sabrina's eyes and laughed. Their reaction disconcerted their female colleague, who snapped, "How does that make you feel?" Then the woman recovered her TV manners and lowered her voice to radiate puzzled concern. "Do you think your thighs were the real problem, or are the rumors of interpersonal differences between you and another contestant true?"

In other words, was Sabrina's body or her personality the bigger loser? Her insides quivered, an outright betrayal of her resolution to get tough on herself. Although she'd learned to handle snarky comments since she'd won the Miss Georgia crown, nothing in her existence to date—her *pampered* existence, as Jake called it—had equipped her to deal with the irrational hostility that insisted her legs had somehow let the state down.

She put a hand to the orchid she'd tucked behind her left ear as she left her dressing room in Vegas. The deep pink flower contrasted nicely with her blond hair and her yellow dress—but so much for the hope it would distract attention from her legs. Dammit, where was Tyler? She wanted to throw her jacket over her head and flee, even though she'd hate for Jake to see her running away.

Behind the reporters, Jake straightened and stepped forward. Sabrina frowned—then, as a camera flashed, hastily raised her eyebrows to smooth her forehead. With her luck, she'd end up in tomorrow's *Journal-*

Constitution looking like a bad-tempered shrew. With fat thighs.

Mentally, she continued to frown at Jake. No one should look that good under fluorescent lighting. His skin had a healthy tan, and when he smiled, his teeth gleamed white.

She did a double take. *Jake, smiling at me?*

Sure, it looked as if he was gritting his teeth—definitely smiling, and definitely at her. He was going to rescue her, she realized, which was even more bizarre.

"Sabrina." Jake's deep, commanding voice swung the crowd in his direction.

Just like that. A potential governor of Georgia obviously held sway over a dumped beauty queen. Now she understood why he was here—he'd seen the opportunity for some free publicity for his election campaign and was cashing in on her thighs.

She took advantage of the distraction to glare at him. Then he arrived at her side, and his presence sucked up all available oxygen, leaving her in a vacuum of awareness. Darn it, she hated that he could still do that to her.

He tugged her heavy carry-on bag off her shoulder. "Are you okay?"

Sabrina blinked at his concern. Before she could reply, he turned to the reporters, who by now were firing questions, and held up a hand.

"If you folks bought into the garbage dished out about Sabrina at the Miss U.S.A. Pageant," Jake said, "then shame on you."

Huh? Sabrina's mouth dropped open. Shouldn't he

be speechifying about the Georgia school system or some other political hot potato?

"Some of you—" he pointed to the reporter from the *Journal-Constitution* and an interviewer from *Good Morning Atlanta* "—went on record six months ago as saying Sabrina Merritt is the most beautiful Miss Georgia ever. Now you're letting a bunch of Yankees tell you otherwise?"

A murmur rose among the shuffling reporters.

The Yankee quip was well judged—Sabrina wished she'd thought of it herself. Because this wasn't Jake's fight. Ironic that the very time she was determined to stand her ground, the man least likely to defend her had an attack of chivalry. "Jake, you don't have to—"

"Take it from me," Jake told the crowd, now swelled by curious travelers and airport personnel, "Sabrina Merritt is a beautiful person inside and out."

Sabrina's famous thighs almost gave way; she steadied herself by clutching at the nearest immovable object. Jake. Through the soft, worn cotton of his casual shirt, she felt the strength of muscle in his forearm.

Jake's gaze flickered, but he kept his focus on the spectators, where a smattering of clapping had broken out. "And," he said in a voice that brooked no argument, "she has amazing legs."

He would know. An unwelcome tide of memory swamped Sabrina. But Jake didn't appear to be in the thrall of their shared history. He bestowed his most charming smile on the photographers. "That's all, folks." To Sabrina, he said in a low voice, "Let's get out of here."

"But Tyler—"

"He's not here, I'm your chauffeur."

"I need to—" A glance at the reporters told her no one wanted to hear her stand up for herself. All the interest was in Jake, who was already shepherding her through the crowd. "I haven't picked up my suitcase," she protested.

"I'll have one of my staff get it."

His black Alfa Romeo was parked right outside the terminal, where only taxis and rental-car shuttles were allowed. Jake paid off the guy minding the Alfa, then held the door open for Sabrina. He jerked his head at her to get in.

"A prospective governor shouldn't park illegally," she said.

"You think that's what'll lose me the primary?" he asked with an irony she didn't understand.

She slid into the car, and a minute later Jake was maneuvering through the stop-start terminal traffic with his usual controlled flair. Sabrina didn't realize she was holding her breath until they passed the Welcome to Atlanta sign on the airport periphery and she let it out.

Jake glanced over at her. "Your skirt's too long."

"Are you kidding? Those guys wanted to make mincemeat out of my thighs." Ugh, the words conjured an unpleasant image; Sabrina squirmed in her seat. "You can't blame me for covering up."

"Avoidance doesn't work. Confronting challenges head-on is the only way to win the respect of the media."

It wasn't the *media's* respect she needed at this stage,

though it might help with her new job. "I was about to *confront* those reporters when you butted in."

He raised his eyebrows. "A simple thank-you will suffice."

"I can fight my own battles," she said, striving for a dignity that would put Jake in his place. *His place* being out of her life.

He snorted. "If you're trying to tell me you're no longer Daddy's helpless little princess…"

Her fingers curled in her lap. "Did you see my father at the airport?" she demanded. "You know, given half a chance, he would have been there, browbeating those guys. I can get past this on my own."

"Why break the habit of a lifetime now?" Visibly, Jake bit down on further criticism. Which wasn't like him. He was the one person who didn't pull his punches with her.

"Why were you at the airport instead of Tyler?" she asked.

"You'll see."

Typical Jake, keeping information to himself, treating her as if she was an infant. And not a very smart one at that. Sabrina feigned a gasp of horror. "You've gone over to the dark side!"

At his impatient look, she elaborated. "You came to save me from those reporters—you've joined the Coddle Sabrina Merritt League."

He rolled his eyes. "Never going to happen, sweetheart."

The *sweetheart* hovered between them. Sabrina tried to think of a smart comment. Then the hard line of

Jake's mouth curved in something that might have been a grimace, but just might have been...

"What's with the weird smile?" she asked. "That's the second one today."

Immediately, his lips resumed their granite set. "Tyler said I had to be nice," he admitted.

Tyler was Jake's cousin. He'd managed to stay close friends with both of them, despite the rift between Jake and Sabrina. She *pffed.* "I don't need Tyler championing my cause, and I don't need you grinning at me."

"My smile is my best feature," Jake said. "Seventy percent of voters think so." Again, that ironic tone.

"A hundred percent of *this* voter doesn't agree." She laced her fingers in her lap. "I count on you being nasty."

They lapsed into a moment's silence as he passed a moving truck. "I'm not nasty."

"Mean, then," she amended. "I rely on you not to handle me with kid gloves. So don't go screwing up my world any more than it already is." She folded her arms and looked out her window at the light industrial area they were passing through.

"So you don't need your dad, you don't need Tyler. Do they know you're flying solo?" He sounded curious rather than sarcastic.

"They'll figure it out when they see the changes I'm making." She twisted to face Jake. "Being Miss Georgia has been an empowering experience."

Another snort—she should have known better than to trust his interest.

"That's what you said on TV," he said, "in Las Vegas."

She pounced. "So you were watching."

The color that rose above the collar of his striped shirt was some compensation.

"I figured it was a line to impress the judges," he said.

Sabrina contemplated how, if that had been her strategy, it had been a dismal failure. "Your defense of me at the airport was very touching," she said, the memory of her humiliation stinging afresh.

"Don't take it personally, I just told the truth. You do have great legs." He turned on the radio, tuned in to a current-affairs show. He'd had enough of this conversation, so apparently it was over.

Sabrina hit the off button; Jake's head jerked in her direction. "I meant," she said, "the bit where you said I'm beautiful inside and out."

His lips clamped together, then parted just enough for him to mutter, "I got carried away with my own rhetoric."

"A common pitfall for politicians."

No reply. Just the jump of a muscle in his cheek as he returned his focus to the road.

The buzz of her cell phone had Sabrina rummaging through her purse. One glance at the display and she stuffed the phone back into the jumble of makeup and tissues.

"Reporter?" Jake asked.

"My father."

"Don't you want to remind him how you don't need him anymore?"

"He'll soon see that." Her dad's impeccable sources would have reached him in Dallas where he was playing golf this weekend. He would know she was back and would be intent on shielding her, comforting her. Yet he would deny with his last breath that he had no respect for his youngest daughter—plenty of love, but no faith in her capabilities. Why had she let him, and everyone else, get away with that attitude for so long?

Sabrina realized Jake had taken a turn away from the direction of Buckhead, the exclusive area of Atlanta where they'd both grown up. "Hey, where are you going?"

"My place."

Her heart jolted, the way it had the first time he'd said those words to her, years ago. "Excuse me?" That came out high, panicky. Because no way could he be planning on doing what they'd done back then. Could he?

"I want to talk to you."

Talk. Sabrina's pulse slowed. Thank goodness he couldn't read her mind.

"Without the risk of one of your sisters barging in," Jake added.

Sabrina swallowed, licked her lips. "You and I don't talk."

Technically, they talked often. Their families were close friends, they met at so many social occasions, it would be impossible to maintain the level of hostility that had consumed them five years ago.

To ease those social connections, they'd fallen into a kind of barbed banter that let them express their dislike in a way that didn't discomfit other people. Everyone knew their history, no one expected them to be pals.

Except Tyler, who, for an intelligent man, had a naive view of their potential for reconciliation.

But they didn't have private, personal conversations— Sabrina couldn't remember when she'd last been alone with Jake. Correction, she *wished* she couldn't remember.

"Don't you think it's time to forgive and forget?" Jake said. "Time we started talking again?"

Jake Warrington, the man who never did anything that didn't serve his ambition, wanted to be friends? She didn't even have to think about it. "Nope, I'm good for a few more years."

His mouth twitched. She looked away. "I want to go home now." *Home.* Sabrina had moved back in with her dad when she won the Miss Georgia title. For her security, her father had insisted. He would argue when she told him she was moving out, but this time she would stand firm.

Jake kept driving in the wrong direction.

"This is kidnapping," she pointed out.

"Only if I ask for a ransom and threaten to cut off your fingers." He accelerated to get through a light before it turned red. "I'll deliver you back to Daddy after we talk."

"Talk about what?"

"I need your help." He made a face, as if the words tasted of arsenic.

What help could Jake possibly need from her? Fashion advice? She slid a glance at him. She couldn't fault his style. He looked fantastic whatever he wore.

He wasn't about to divulge more. Short of wrenching the steering wheel out of his hands—and she would never, *ever* knowingly do something that might cause another accident—Sabrina had no choice but to go with him. She tipped her head back against the headrest and closed her eyes.

When it became obvious Sabrina wasn't about to argue, Jake relaxed his grip on the wheel. He caught himself watching her out of the corner of his eye. That flower in her hair, the orchid, made him think about his father and that in turn made him think about all his problems. He dropped his gaze to the graceful curve of Sabrina's neck, then lower. *Don't go there.* He forced his attention back to the road. Any guy would find her a distraction. From a beautiful, slightly skinny twenty-one-year-old, she'd grown into a stunning woman with curves that made his hands itch. An itch he planned to ignore.

SABRINA SPENT THE remainder of the journey to Virginia Highlands shoring up her resolution. Whatever Jake needed, she wasn't the one to help him. The distance between them might be all about hostility on his side, but on hers it was self-preservation. Jake had broken her heart five years ago. Just looking at him reminded her of a pain she didn't want to revisit, a vulnerability she never wanted to succumb to again.

Jake flicked his turn signal and pulled into the driveway of a house that blended modern design and rustic materials—stone base, natural cedar siding, cedar-shingle roof—to stunning effect. Sabrina had never been here before, but she'd heard all about it. The reality was even more impressive. She buzzed her window down, stuck her head out. "This place is fantastic."

"Built by Warrington Construction."

She knew from Tyler, whose brother Max ran Warrington Construction, that the basic design was Jake's, handed over to an architect for refining.

Jake walked around the car to open Sabrina's door. He hadn't opened a door for her in years. "What's going on, Jake? I don't trust you when you're nice."

"Welcome to my world," he muttered.

She climbed out, pushed a strand of hair back behind her ear as she looked up at the house.

Jake's scanned her, head to toe. "Inside," he ordered.

The sooner she heard him out, the sooner she could go home and get on with her life. Sabrina stuck her chin in the air and marched up the front walk.

Jake keyed in an entry code and the extra-high, double-wide front door swung silently, easily, on industrial-size hinges.

Sabrina stepped into a slate-floored atrium, glanced at the elaborately framed mirror on the far wall, then up to the ceiling. "This is beautiful."

"Thanks." He led the way to the open-plan living and dining area, dominated by a stone-and-timber fireplace. Recesses in the fire surround stored logs and pinecones. Rustic.

"The kitchen's through here." Jake pointed to the doorway beyond.

She followed him into the large, south-facing kitchen. Afternoon sunlight streamed in through the French doors, making patterns on the white marble floor and the warm wooden cabinets.

"Have a seat." Jake waved to the stools at the marble-topped island. He filled the kettle and put it on the stove.

"You must love living here, in a place you've created for yourself," Sabrina said as he retrieved mugs, coffee, sugar.

He shrugged. "I wanted to build something distinctive, but with an architectural integrity that would stand the test of time."

Typical of Jake to reduce this incredible home to something as calculated as *architectural integrity*. They lapsed into a silence while they waited for the kettle.

At last, Jake concentrated on adding boiling water to the French press. He added half-and-half and one sugar to Sabrina's cup, nothing to his, then poured the dark, rich brew. He slid hers across the island.

Sabrina blew on the hot coffee then took a sip. She gave him the thumbs-up and a mischievous smile. "Perfect."

Jake's scowl told her he wished he hadn't remembered how she took hers. He reached for the folder on the end of the island and handed her a sheet of paper. "Read this."

Curious enough to obey, she put her mug down on the island. She scanned the page, a summary of the latest opinion poll about the forthcoming gubernatorial primary. "Ouch."

"Exactly," he said. "The public trust me about as much as they'd trust an arsonist with a match."

She gripped the paper more tightly. "You must have known that would be a problem."

"Know why they don't trust me?" His tone was conversational, but she picked up the old resentment beneath the surface.

Sabrina swallowed, though she hadn't drunk any more coffee. "Because your father broke the law."

His mouth tightened. "If you could do it over again," he said, "would you?"

They both knew what "it" was. The back of her neck prickled; she dropped the damning opinion-poll results. "Jake, your father was a hero to me, the best governor a man could be. I thought he was so caring, so principled." Needlessly, she stirred her coffee. "No one could have been more upset to discover he'd taken a bribe— apart from his family," she added quickly. "But no matter how much I admired him, I couldn't let him get away with it."

"I mean," Jake said deliberately, "would you do it the same way?"

He had her there. Because with the benefit of hindsight— and a whole lot more maturity—she wouldn't have been so rash in her denunciation of Governor Ted Warrington. Wouldn't have made those distraught calls summoning the media to a midnight press conference, thus guaranteeing the story would trounce every other headline off the front pages. She wouldn't have forced Jake and his family to wake up to a posse of reporters on their doorstep, so that his dad appeared before the nation aging and vulnerable in his pajamas.

She didn't want to think about that night, or about what happened afterward—the public frenzy that had condemned Ted before he gave his side of the story. And the flaming, bitter end of her relationship with Jake.

"The outcome would have been the same," she said uneasily, not meeting his eyes. She caught her reflection in the oven door, saw how she'd hunched down in self-defense. She straightened on her stool. "Your father would still have had to quit."

"People might at least have given him credit for having selfless motives. If he'd been allowed to retain some dignity..." He let out a hiss. "My parents' marriage might have survived."

She drew in a pained breath. If he dared suggest that had his parents not divorced, his mom would never have dated the man who'd taken her sailing on a day when no right-thinking person would have gone out, and drowned them both...

Sabrina shuddered—and saw from Jake's narrowed eyes that she was taking exactly the path he wanted her to. Fortunately, he brought out her fighting instincts like nobody else. "Whatever help you want from me," she said coolly, "you obviously think you need to guilt-trip me first. Let's consider that done, and you can tell me why I'm here."

He blinked. He must have expected her to cave at the first hint of conflict. She could practically see him re-arranging his tactics.

"I need your help to establish public confidence in me," he said finally, matching her bluntness.

"How could I—" That's when realization dawned. "Ah. You mean, like—" she waggled her fingers, quote marks for an imaginary headline "—Fat-Thighed Beauty Queen Says, Vote Warrington?"

"I mean—" he made quote marks of his own "—Whistle-blower Says Son Is Not Like Father."

She had to admit, it had a certain poetic beauty. If the woman who'd blown the whistle on crooked Governor Ted Warrington endorsed Ted's son for office, voters would have to believe Jake was on the level. But the thought of getting involved with him again, even politically...

"I don't understand why you're even running for office," she hedged. "You knew this would be a problem."

"Susan did some polling before I decided to run. The results suggested that my grandfather's and great-uncle's years of public service to the state were enough to outweigh Dad's mistakes." Susan Warrington, Jake's aunt and Tyler's mom, was Jake's campaign manager, as she'd been his father's before him. Jake came from a long line of Georgia governors. "None of the numbers we've polled since then support that conclusion," he finished.

Sabrina tapped the page in front of her. "That tells me why you thought you could win. You still haven't said why you want to be governor." Jake had always thought bigger than Georgia; he'd had his heart set on national politics, starting with Congress, back when he and Sabrina were dating.

The bribe scandal had ended that ambition. Jake had quit politics to work with Max at Warrington Construction.

"My father cheated this state, and I want to put that

right," he said. "I want to move on. I'm sick of being 'crooked Ted Warrington's son.'"

Sabrina swallowed and ducked her head. The poll data caught her eye. "This isn't all bad news. People think you're intelligent, likable and—and you have a nice smile." According to the demographics data at the bottom of the page, seventy percent of the respondents were women. Sabrina knew they meant his smile—the one that adorned campaign posters around town, the one she never saw—was *sexy*. "Maybe Susan's original numbers were right, and people will look past what your dad did."

"They won't," he said flatly.

"My support would be more of a handicap than a help," she assured him. "You saw those photographers at the airport. I'm a bad joke."

He barked a laugh. "I guess you haven't seen the local papers. The media might be poking fun at you, but there's been a swell of public sympathy like you wouldn't believe. The newspapers are full of letters saying what a wonderful Miss Georgia you are. And you're Saint Sabrina of Talkback Radio." The sweep of his hand encompassed the Georgia airwaves.

"You're exaggerating," she said, a part of her hoping he wasn't. That the entire state didn't hold her in contempt.

"Sabrina." Jake gripped the edge of the island. "Would you trust me as governor?"

She would never trust him with her heart again, and would recommend no other woman should, either, but she did trust him as a politician. Unlike his father's, Jake's integrity was unshakable.

"Yes," she said.

"Then we don't have a problem." His fingers relaxed. "Do we?"

She almost agreed. Then she realized what Jake was doing. In short order, he'd had her feeling grateful for his intervention at the airport, sorry for him over his poll results, guilty about the role she'd played in his family's breakup... He was manipulating her emotions, just as he had five years ago. Back then, he'd left her shattered. Thankfully, he'd been too mad to see how he'd hurt her.

"Your getting involved in the governor race will take everyone's minds off your legs," he coaxed, as if offering her an irresistible enticement.

"Politics being even weightier?" she said sharply.

He grinned, almost amicably, and she guessed he thought her agreement was in the bag.

"I need you to tell the world you have complete trust in me," he said. "And to attend some of my campaign events between now and the primary vote in June. We could start Monday—I'm opening an art exhibition at Wellesley High School. Your dad will probably be there, his firm is one of the sponsors. You could come along. What do you say?"

Sabrina studied her fingernails to avoid the compelling pressure of his gaze. "I say no."

CHAPTER TWO

JAKE SHOVED HIMSELF off his stool and took a couple of paces away from the island. "No to the high school art show?"

"No to all of it," Sabrina said. *No, I'm not dumb enough to get sucked into helping a guy who knows exactly how to reel me in.* She cringed at the thought of how he'd led her to this moment today. *Sabrina Merritt is a beautiful person, inside and out.* Jake knew her looks were the source of her confidence, and he'd pandered to that. It felt just like the old days, when he'd played on her vulnerability to dissuade her from reporting his father the moment she'd learned of the bribe. What next? Would he try to use the attraction that still shimmered in the air between them, the heat that rose above their enmity?

"Dammit, Sabrina," he said. "I'm not letting you out of here until you agree to help."

She pressed her right hand palm down onto the island, slid it toward him. "Is this where you chop off my fingers for the ransom note?"

His gaze dropped to her manicured, Crushed Raspberry nails. "Just tell me why," he said tightly.

"I have plans for my future, and they don't involve revisiting the past."

For long seconds he processed that. "When you say plans, do you mean like your plan to climb Everest?"

That stung. "When I said that, I was back on my feet for the first time after the accident." She hated thinking about the car crash that had killed her mom and left Sabrina, then still a teenager, unable to walk for eighteen months. She glared at Jake. "Cut me some slack, will you?"

"Like you cut my father some slack?" he retorted.

The animosity between them was a tangible beast, provoked in an instant, snuffling at territory they hadn't explored in years. Sabrina found herself shaking. Jake touched her hand and said, "Sorry, I shouldn't have mentioned the Everest thing."

It was safest to assume his remorse was prompted by concern for his campaign. She pulled her hand back, rubbing the spot he'd left tingling. "You always were a know-it-all jerk," she grumbled.

His shoulders eased. "You always were a spoiled brat," he returned. He sat back down on his stool. "What's your plan, Sabrina?"

"I don't have to tell you. I haven't even told Dad yet."

"So it's something he won't like," he speculated. He knew how close she was to her father. "Does it involve liposuction?"

"Of course not." Her hands went involuntarily to her thighs. "There's nothing wrong with my legs."

"A point I made on your behalf today," he reminded her.

She knew he was manipulating her again, but it wouldn't hurt to tell him. "I've lined up a job with the Injured Kids Education Trust."

He drained his cup. "Never heard of it."

"The trust aims to establish a dedicated school for kids who've suffered serious injuries. It'll combine physical rehabilitation with a regular high school education in a social environment. I met one of the directors through Tyler—the foundation funds their operating costs." Tyler was the president of the charitable Warrington Foundation.

"I approached the trust a couple of months ago to ask if I could get involved. They want me to be their front person, to promote the need for the school and help lobby for funding. I had to get the Miss U.S.A. Pageant out of the way," she said, "but the trust plans to announce my appointment this week."

"Why haven't you told your dad?" Jake cleared their cups away.

"Dad still wants me to work at Merritt, Merritt & Finch with him. Every time I suggest another job, he comes up with ten reasons why I should be somewhere he can look out for me, even though I'm not qualified to do anything in a law firm beyond opening the mail. He's driving me crazy."

Jake's eyes narrowed. "You love being pampered and protected by your father."

Jake Warrington, The Man Who Knew Too Much. He knew she'd been born with an extra dependency gene that was the perfect match for her father's extra protectiveness gene.

Jake had neither defect. Sabrina looked at him, at the broad shoulders that could bear the problems of a dozen chunky-thighed beauty queens, then at the uncompromising jaw that warned against leaning on him.

She wished she'd heeded that warning five years ago.

"I don't love it anymore," she said.

"You've never held down a job longer than six months. How is this different from any of your other one-minute-wonder careers?" Jake leaned back precariously on his stool. "From, say, cordon bleu catering, or your burning ambition to join the police?"

"Neither of those was right for me, but I know this is."

"Then there was, let me see…" He rubbed his chin. "Dog-grooming school?"

Did he plan to catalog all the career choices she'd embraced and abandoned with equal speed? "That was over summer vacation, and I was trying to make a point to my father."

The point being that, unlike her sisters, she didn't want to pursue a law degree. Her father had finally conceded the point, but his latest idea was that she should work at the family firm while she trained to be a paralegal.

"What about your job in Congressman Smith's office, working for world peace?" A sneer in the words. "At least that used your political science degree."

"My degree is in international relations." Didn't he remember even that much about her?

"You mean, that Swiss guy you dated in your final year?"

She scowled. "Funny." But since she'd chosen international relations specifically because the course wasn't as tough as political science, then just scraped by while her social life took off exponentially, she wasn't on firm ground. "Congressman Smith gave me the job as a favor to Dad, so I'd have something to talk about at the Miss U.S.A. Pageant. It was only ever a part-time, short-term project, not something I wanted to make a career out of. World peace is overrated." It had been mentioned countless times at the Miss U.S.A. Pageant, the most warlike environment she'd ever encountered.

"And you think you can metamorphose into someone who's serious about her work?" Jake's stool scraped on the floor as he stood. "I can see why you're attracted to this injury-trust idea, but admit it, Sabrina, the chances you'll stick with it are low to zero."

He wouldn't be the last person to say that. Sabrina stood, too, robbing him of the height advantage.

"Your opinion is irrelevant," she said. "I'm twenty-six years old, and I've finally found an opportunity that will let me be more than Jonah Merritt's pampered youngest daughter, the one who had the accident." There was a time when she'd thought Jake saw past that label, but she'd been proven wrong. "This is a fresh start for me."

It might have been a moment's sympathy that softened Jake's blue eyes, but more likely it was a trick of the light, because when he spoke, his voice was harsh. "I want a fresh start, too. Warringtons have served this state as governor for generations, until my father screwed up. I can't wipe the slate clean unless I win this primary. If I can just do that, I'll be a shoo-in for governor—the party will swing its full support behind me, and it hasn't lost an election in Georgia in fifty years."

His hands curled into fists, as if he had to squeeze out his next words. "Please, Sabrina, help me."

Like her, he wanted to put the past behind him. Despite their mutual dislike, Sabrina sympathized. *Don't let him get to you.* She wrapped her arms around her middle. "The days when I fell over my feet in my rush to do whatever you wanted are long gone, Jake."

What the hell did that mean? Jake paced to the French doors, then turned to face her. "If you fell over your feet, that was your choice. I didn't ask you to." He couldn't suppress his outrage, even though logic told him to stay calm. Back when they were dating, he'd indeed known she would do anything for him, and been careful to ask for nothing. Until the bribe. And look how well that had turned out.

"You didn't have to ask. I did whatever it took to please you. But I'm stronger now, stronger than you or anyone knows."

The disconnect between what she was saying and her appearance couldn't have been greater, Jake thought. Sabrina might not be as skinny as some of her rivals at Miss U.S.A., but there was something about her that suggested fragility. Her wrists were slender, her fingers long and fine. She had a habit of shielding her clear blue eyes with her lashes, so that people—men—worried about her.

Since their breakup, Jake always assumed she was hiding her laughter at the way they made idiots of themselves over her.

The way he almost had. The only good to come out of her betrayal was that it had forced an end to a relationship that teetered on the verge of out of control but that he hadn't quite been able to bring himself to abandon.

He hauled his mind back to the present, to Sabrina standing hands on hips in front of him. "Okay, I believe you," he said. "You're strong. And I accept that you're dedicated to your new job—in fact, I admire that."

She didn't relax one iota.

"But your responsibilities for the trust don't sound like full-time work. Surely you can help me out with the occasional interview, a couple of public appearances?"

She was shaking her head before he finished talking.

"Dammit, Sabrina, you're not the one who should be holding a grudge here," he snapped. She was famous among their friends for her generous willingness to give people the benefit of the doubt, a second chance. Why should he be the exception to the rule? Unless...

"This isn't about you and me, our personal relationship, is it?" He grasped her shoulders, and the contact with bare flesh, covered only by the thin straps of her dress, shocked him with the power of a lightning strike. He jerked backward, at the same moment as she wrenched herself free. Jake willed his breathing to slow down. "Are you refusing to help me because you're still mad that I dumped you?"

Damn, damn, damn. What was it about Sabrina that destroyed his rationality? Now he'd made her mad.

She pressed her full lips together as she snatched her purse. "I'm leaving."

Jake recognized that stubbornness. The last time he'd seen it, she'd been in the hospital, not much more than a kid, fighting to recover from the accident with everything she had.

Years later when he'd been drawn against all good sense to Sabrina the Social Butterfly, he'd concluded that her recovery must have drained the reserves of her strength, her courage. Which explained why she was content to accept, almost welcomed people's stifling protectiveness and concern. He'd understood, sympathized…though not to the extent that he'd let her pull her helpless act on him.

Now, he realized that teenage obstinacy had just been shelved until she needed it. And he was at a disconcerting loss as to what to do next. No more begging, that was for sure. He would think of something else. Tomorrow. He grabbed his keys. "I'll drive you home."

"I'll call Tyler, have him pick me up."

If Jake hadn't felt so bitter, he'd have laughed. She expected him to believe her refusal was about her new start, nothing to do with their personal history. He held out the phone to her. "Here you go, Miss Independence. Summon Tyler to your rescue."

He watched as she blushed beet red. Wordlessly, she took the phone from him. Her finger hovered over the buttons, then she dialed.

She ordered a cab.

Too little, too late, Jake thought as they waited in silence for the taxi. Which they both knew would take her to her father's house. Sabrina could claim the independence of a yeti. But she was still the same old Sabrina, relying on her looks and on her family and friends to get her through life's difficulties.

And if she was the same old Sabrina, one way or another, he would convince her to do what he wanted.

"SABRINA, THANKS FOR rearranging your schedule to meet with us this afternoon." Richard Ainsley, head of the Injured Kids Education Trust, shook Sabrina's hand and ushered her into his luxurious penthouse apartment.

"No problem, you know the trust is my top priority." Sabrina smiled at the man who had sufficient belief in her abilities that he'd offered her the job of her dreams. In her new role, she would do so much to help children and teens with spinal and other serious injuries. To give them hope. Nothing could be more worthwhile.

The tension of yesterday's conversation with Jake faded with each step she took across the plush, cream-colored carpet.

She just wished she was a little more wide-awake for this meeting. Behind Richard's back, she stifled a yawn. She shouldn't have wasted precious sleep time last night tossing and turning, worrying about Jake's election prospects. She'd bet he hadn't given *her* career another thought.

Sleep deprivation must be the reason why it took a while for Richard's exact words to seep into her brain. "Uh, did you say, to meet with *us?*" As far as she knew, this get-together was an informal one-on-one meeting to draft an announcement of her appointment.

Over his shoulder he said, "A couple of the other board members are joining us."

"A couple" meant four, Sabrina discovered when she followed Richard into the dining room. A silver-haired woman, a slightly younger brunette and two middle-aged men were already seated at the antique mahogany table.

Was it her imagination, or did four pairs of eyes drop to her thighs?

Richard introduced her to the board members. Focused on clenching her thigh muscles in an attempt to minimize their bulk, Sabrina struggled to absorb their names.

Richard pulled out a green velvet-upholstered chair for her, the other side of the table from the others. He took his seat at the head, which meant she now had five people staring at her. Outranked by age, number and severity of demeanor, Sabrina felt like a five-year-old who'd flunked Finger Painting 101.

"I'm honored that the announcement of my appointment was important enough to bring you all here." She laughed nervously.

Richard didn't offer her coffee, the way he had at previous meetings—Sabrina looked longingly at the pot on the sideboard. Behind the coffee, through glass-fronted cabinet doors, she saw an array of spirits. A stiff whiskey held sudden appeal.

"You'll remember," Richard began, "my mentioning that your appointment would need to be ratified by the board."

"I recall your describing it as a formality," she said.

His gaze slid away. Sabrina got a hollow feeling behind her ribs.

Maybe because she'd just had her first personal conversation with Jake in five years, a saying of his father's popped into her head. *If you want orchids, don't plant camellias.*

If she wanted this job, she couldn't afford to joke, or to skirt around the topic.

"Is there a problem with my appointment?" Sabrina asked. "Because I am one hundred percent committed to the trust and to what you're—*we're*—trying to do. As you said, Richard, my past injuries and my public profile make me the ideal candidate."

Richard's mouth pulled back in a smile that was more grimace, as if he didn't appreciate her excellent memory. "The board's thinking with regard to public profile has, uh, changed. We're now thinking of a specific *kind* of profile." He sent a silent appeal to his colleagues.

The silver-haired woman spoke up. "The Injured Kids Education Trust is at a crucial juncture."

So is my life.

Silver Hair continued, "With the election coming up, this is our big chance to lobby for funds for the school and to create awareness at the local and national levels. We believe we need a front person with more—" her gazed flicked to the table, as if she could see right through the mahogany to Sabrina's thighs "—gravitas."

She raised her eyebrows, perhaps questioning whether Sabrina knew what *gravitas* meant.

"You think being Miss Georgia means I don't have gravitas?" Sabrina asked.

One of the men cleared his throat. "It's more that we wouldn't expect our spokesperson to be front-page news in the tabloid newspapers."

The man next to him fingered the knot in his navy-blue silk tie. "The rumors of physical confrontation in Las Vegas…"

"The only confrontation was verbal, when another competitor said she wanted to slap me." Sabrina shifted on her chair; it was mortifying to have to explain Miss Maine's sudden conviction that Sabrina's wealthy father must have bribed the judges for her to win the Miss Georgia contest. Just because nearly every other woman had worked her way up through contests like Miss Save 'n' Grow Bank Summer Carnival before making it at state level…

Distaste crossed Richard's face.

"She said it," Sabrina said levelly. "I walked away and that was the end of it."

"Not as far as the media were concerned," Silver Hair pointed out. "The public perception is of a squabble."

The temperature in the room seemed to have plunged to arctic levels. Sabrina shivered in her pink silk blouse and tailored knee-length cream skirt, perfect, she'd thought this morning, in their demureness. Maybe something severe and black would have been a better choice. She rubbed her arms. This was how Jake must feel, poised to lose the primary.

But she knew for sure Jake wasn't about to give up on becoming governor just because she wouldn't cooperate.

I won't give up, either. Sabrina drew a steadying breath and willed herself not to react in a way that might shred the board's paper-thin respect for her.

"My level of public support has actually grown since the incidents you mention," she said. Jake's comments had checked out in the online search she'd run last night. She had a lot of new fans since the Miss U.S.A. debacle.

"We're not looking for someone who can whip up the sympathy of the man in the street," Silver Hair said. "We need to impress legislators, educators, corporate sponsors. People with serious concerns."

"I'm pleased you said that." Sabrina shot her a dazzling smile. "Because people with serious concerns don't pay much attention to tabloid headlines. The media will soon lose interest in my, uh, deficiencies. What won't change is that I'm the best fit for this job." She squared her shoulders as she glanced around the table. "Do you think you'll find another spokesperson with my public recognition at *all* levels of society, who knows what it's like to put an education on hold because of an injury? Someone who truly understands the difference our school will make?"

Richard leafed through the papers in front of him as if he had two dozen such candidates right there in black and white.

Sabrina knew he didn't. She breathed a little easier and spread her fingers on the table's polished surface. It was natural that the board should have questions about the headlines. What mattered was that she could show them she was unique.

"The other possibility," the man in the blue tie said, "is that we recruit a family member of someone affected by serious injury. Someone who can talk about the effect on the entire family."

"It lacks the same emotional impact," Sabrina said with all the authority she could muster.

"Perhaps, but that person might have other qualities that lend themselves to the job. More orthodox qualities."

Sabrina's spine tingled. "Do you have someone in mind?"

"One of the reasons I welcomed your approach," Richard said, "was because your father's firm has a strong track record fighting legal battles in the education system."

Okay, maybe she was as stupid as they appeared to think, because it took a full five seconds for Sabrina to see where this was going.

"*My* family? You're thinking one of my *sisters* could front the trust?"

She would rather they gave the job to Miss Maine. To not only have her dream snatched from her, but then to see it handed to one of her fearsomely intelligent, supersuccessful sisters…

I won't let them do this.

"It's only a thought," Richard said.

Sabrina whisked her trembling hands into her lap, and was embarrassed to see her fingertips had left ten smudges on the glossy tabletop. "Neither of my sisters would dream of accepting the position," she said. "Not when they know how important it is to me."

She hoped she was right. Her sisters loved her, but they'd thought her winning Miss Georgia and the gusto with which she'd thrown herself into the role was cute, rather than a worthy achievement. They didn't take her seriously, and she knew darned well they didn't respect her. Why should they?

She'd spent years letting people do things for her because they'd worried she would overdo it in the aftermath of the accident. Had a string of unlikely, unfulfilled ambitions, culminating in the ignominy of the Miss U.S.A. Pageant. And now the injured children she wanted to help would have to rely on someone else to champion them. To think, she'd even imagined announcing her new role to her family and, yes, impressing them.

She didn't really believe either of her sisters would snatch the job out from under her if she asked them not to. But she was glad she hadn't told them about the appointment, glad she didn't have to witness their lack of surprise when they learned she'd been fired before she started.

Jake wouldn't be surprised, either. He was about to be proven right—she couldn't hold down a job.

The only person who believes in me is me. The thought left an unpleasant, metallic taste in her mouth.

If I'm the only person who believes in me, I'm the only person who can fix this.

Okay, she hadn't expected establishing her independence and earning some respect to be so fraught. But she couldn't give up now. "The problem with a knee-jerk reaction to the headlines," she said, interrupting Silver Hair, who'd started pontificating about credibility, "is that it fails to take some important considerations into account."

"And those are...?" Richard prompted.

At last, someone was giving her a break. She smiled at him, more warmly than he deserved. "You don't just need someone to recite whatever words you put in their mouth. You need someone who'll have active input into your strategy."

Sabrina spread her palms on the table again, not caring if she perspired right through the wood's high-gloss polish. "For instance, you're relying on the education department and a few private backers to open their wallets to build the school. That's not good enough." Richard's chin jutted at her temerity, but she didn't stop. "The school should be fully state funded, so we don't go through the cycle year after year of begging for donations. We need backing at the highest level of the state legislature."

Silver Hair let out a condescending laugh. "That's the dream scenario, but it's not going to happen. Certainly not because of your involvement."

The woman's rudeness was breathtaking.

Spots floated before Sabrina's eyes. She hadn't felt this angry since a resident physician had told her she'd likely never walk again.

She needed to say something to shut these people up, once and for all. Something big, no half measures.

Her high profile and her medical history wouldn't cut it. She needed something that would trump her sisters' brains, business connections and lobbying capabilities.

What would Jake do? Just yesterday, he'd asked a woman he despised to endorse him. A desperate measure. *Jake would do whatever it takes.*

Jake.

Desperation.

"You're probably aware that Jake Warrington, my—" Sabrina drew a shuddery breath "—my *fiancé,* is running for governor."

Every person in the room sat up straighter. Including Sabrina, who was fighting the instinct to slink down in her seat.

"You and Jake Warrington are engaged?" Silver Hair asked.

"He asked me to marry him yesterday." Incredible how easily the lie tripped off her tongue. But then, Jake always said she spoke before she thought.

Richard addressed the board members. "You might have seen Warrington on the TV news, meeting Sabrina at the airport."

"There hasn't been anything in the papers about you and Warrington, uh, being involved," one of the men said.

"We've been discreet." *So discreet, Jake doesn't even know about it.* "You may recall that Jake and I have a, er, troubled past." Heads nodded—anyone who'd been in Georgia during the Warrington bribe scandal knew Ted Warrington's son's girlfriend, working as an intern in the governor's office, had broken the story. "We wanted to be sure of our feelings."

"So, as Warrington's fiancée…" Richard prompted, losing interest in the romantic details.

"Jake fully supports the idea of state funding for the school," she said. "Education is his main campaign platform." At last, the truth! "So our school will be very much on his agenda."

"He's not exactly the fron-trunner in the election," Silver Hair pointed out.

"Jake's commitment to education will put pressure on the other candidates throughout the campaign." That sounded convincing, to Sabrina's ears, at least. "Special-needs education will be on the political agenda whether the others like it or not. If they won't make the same commitment as Jake, they'll look hard-hearted. Kids with severe injuries are an emotional issue—every parent dreads their child being in an accident."

"Good point," Richard said.

"As his fiancée," Sabrina continued, "I'll be on the campaign trail with him. That is, as far as my commitments to the Injured Kids Education Trust allow." She smiled brightly. "I'll be meeting people who are in a position to support the school, and I'll be doing my utmost to convince them."

Any more and she risked betraying her ignorance of Jake's campaign. Sabrina sat back and waited.

Significant glances fired across the room. Richard picked up his pen, made a few notes. He cleared his throat. "The board would like to—"

Yes!

"—congratulate you on your engagement," he said.

Sabrina held her breath as the earlier contempt evolved into congratulatory murmurs.

"I think we're all in agreement—" Richard looked around, received emphatic nods in reply "—that this news changes our perspective."

Sabrina tried not to feel insulted. It didn't matter if they were impressed because she was engaged to Jake. What mattered was that she could do this job.

"We would be delighted if you would come on board as spokesperson for the trust," Richard said.

Her exultant whoop took the directors aback. She toned it down to an emphatic nod. "I would be delighted to accept."

Smiles and handshakes followed, with the men taking the opportunity to kiss a beauty queen.

"This calls for a drink." Richard crossed to the sideboard. "I have a rather fine single malt here." He tilted the bottle in her direction.

Now he brings out the whiskey.

"Not for me." The enormity of what she'd done was starting to sink in, and Sabrina's knees began to shake. One sip of single malt and she'd be laid out on the floor.

The oblivion was tempting. But she was responsible for her own future now. She stretched her mouth into a smile. "I need to tell Jake the good news."

CHAPTER THREE

THE BEAUTY QUEEN'S instruction manual was conspicuously silent on the protocol for telling a man who hates you that he's now your fiancé.

Which meant Sabrina had to figure out her own way to tell Jake, and to enlist his support. Soon. The trust planned to announce her appointment tomorrow, and although she'd emphasized to the directors that her engagement wasn't yet public, was in fact totally secret, one of them was bound to let slip what was apparently her highest qualification for the job.

As soon as she left Richard's penthouse, she called Jake's campaign office from the sanctuary of her lime-green VW Beetle. A staff member told her Jake had a couple of media interviews this afternoon, after which he would go directly to the senior art exhibition at Wellesley High, a private school in Buckhead.

The staffer gave her Jake's cell-phone number, but his phone was switched off. Sabrina left a couple of urgent but non-specific messages. Though she kept her phone close as she ran errands around town, he didn't call back. You'd think he'd return calls from the woman who held his political future in her hands… The thought of wielding so much power cheered Sabrina as she walked into Happy Hands for her five-o'clock manicure appointment.

"You poor sweetie." Tina, the manicurist, hugged Sabrina. "Vile reporters, saying those things about you."

"I'm over it," Sabrina told her as she settled into the chair and immersed her hands in a steaming bowl of scented water. "I'm moving on."

"Good girl." Tina chatted for a minute about the evening dresses worn at the Miss U.S.A. Pageant, then patted Sabrina's hands dry with a soft towel. She pumped some moisturizer into her palms, and began massaging it into Sabrina's skin. "What color today? Scarlet Woman?"

Sabrina flinched. "Make it Lilac Surprise."

Surprise was perhaps an understatement for how Jake would feel about her announcement. But he couldn't get too mad, not when their engagement would help him.

She just needed to tell him about it before anyone else did. He'd invited her to attend the high school exhibition, and that was what she would do.

Sabrina tipped her head back, closed her eyes and tried to plan what she would say.

Despite Tina's relaxing ministrations, the forty-five minutes Sabrina spent at Happy Hands weren't as productive as she'd have liked. Her mind persisted in playing out scenarios that left her…nervous.

She could see herself telling Jake about the engagement, burying the *E* word discreetly within the wonderful news that she was willing to support him for governor. Unfortunately, she couldn't envisage Jake's gratitude. It seemed more probable that his laser mind would zoom in on the fiancé thing and...mostly, the scenarios ended with him strangling her and burying her in a shallow grave. *Yikes.*

THE WELLESLEY HIGH art exhibition and auction was an annual event that attracted a strong turnout from the Buckhead locals, many of whose children were current or former students at the school. Several professional artists, some of them quite well-known, had donated works that hung alongside the teenagers'. The school probably hoped to raise tens of thousands of dollars from tonight's soiree.

Sabrina still hadn't heard from Jake as she wandered through the growing crowd. The official opening was at seven-thirty. It was seven now, and there was no sign of the guest of honor.

Maybe he was picking up his date. Sabrina almost dropped her smoked-salmon canapé. Did Jake have a girlfriend? She popped the canapé into her mouth, where it promptly turned to cardboard. A girlfriend would complicate matters, to put it mildly.

Tyler would have told her if Jake was seeing someone, he always did. As if he worried she might be hurt at the unexpected sight of Jake with another woman.

Sabrina tugged at her dress to make sure it hadn't ridden up on her hips. She'd dressed for tonight with expert attention to her appearance—the one thing she was invariably good at. Her knee-length white silk shift dress, its high collar threaded with gold and silver, was very classy. Lots of gravitas.

Perfect for the spokesperson of a charitable trust. Or for a governor's fiancée.

She abandoned her mineral water and accepted a glass of chardonnay from one of the school's senior students acting as servers.

Several people greeted her, mostly friends of her father's. Her dad should be here, too. He'd gone straight to his office when he flew in from Dallas this morning, which meant so far, she'd been spared a rehashing of the chunky-thighs fiasco.

Sabrina made the requisite small talk, but with more difficulty than usual. With every passing minute her sense of urgency grew.

She sipped her wine, but the excellent vintage, which she knew should taste peachy with a hint of oak, might as well have been antifreeze. She paid scant attention to the artworks people pointed out to her. The exhibition was titled Climb; students had been asked to create paintings or sculptures on the theme of upward movement. Maybe it was a good omen, she thought in an attempt to be positive, of the direction her career and Jake's were about to go.

She was talking to Duncan Frith, the school principal, when she saw Jake shouldering his way through the throng. At first glance he looked ultracivilized—not to mention gorgeous—in his dark custom-made suit and white shirt. Every woman in the place followed him with her eyes. As he neared her, Sabrina realized his expression was thunderous, his mouth set in a grim line that promised zero tolerance for accidental announcements of impending nuptials.

He knows.

His eyes found her, and she had the sense of being lined up in a rifle's sights. Even as her brain reminded her she needed to speak to him, the instincts honed by a lifetime of pampering told her to run. She would grow up and take responsibility next week.

She'd barely managed to maneuver around Duncan's considerable girth, when her elbow was clamped in a viselike grip and Jake muttered, "Oh no you don't."

"Jake!" She pinned a bright, sociable smile to her lips, while her eyes clung to her destination, the red fire-exit sign gleaming at the back of the room. No longer an option, she conceded reluctantly.

"Jake, glad you could make it." Duncan Frith shook Jake's free hand then consulted his watch. "We have ten minutes until the official speeches—let me get you a drink."

"I need a word with Sabrina first." Jake tugged her arm.

She could almost smell the damp earth of the shallow grave. She would be insane to go anywhere with him. "Duncan was just telling me how about the senior history curriculum, and it reminded me of your encyclopedic knowledge of Georgia state history." Under the circumstances, a touch of flattery could do no harm.

"Geography," Duncan corrected her tolerantly. "We were talking about geography."

Jake growled. "Excuse us, Duncan."

Without waiting for a reply, he dragged Sabrina toward the far end of the room, where a cordon marked the end of the exhibition.

She glanced over her shoulder, but didn't see any gorgeous, sophisticated woman in their wake. "Did you bring a date?" she asked.

He paused in his Neanderthal dragging. "Why do you ask?"

"Neither did I. Rather a coincidence," she chirped, "that you and I should be single at the same time. Usually one of us is dating and the other…" She trailed off. Not only was she babbling, a habit Jake despised, but she was also revealing that she paid attention to his love life.

He unclipped the cordon, pushed her through and clipped the velvet rope behind them again. As barriers went, it did little to separate them from the masses… So why did Sabrina feel as if Jake had her alone on a precipice?

"Why did a Richard Ainsley call my campaign office and ask Susan when I plan to announce my support for his school for injured kids?" he demanded. "I assume that's the school you work for."

Sabrina's mind raced. "Er…was that all Richard said?"

"What else might he have said?" Jake asked silkily.

She took a slug of wine. "Did he mention my, uh, relationship with you?"

"Relationship?" Jake frowned. "No." Then, just as Sabrina relaxed, he snapped, "Unless you mean our *engagement!*"

Sabrina took a step backward. "I can explain."

"Tell it to my campaign manager," he said grimly. "I've spent the past half hour convincing an ecstatic Susan there's no engagement. I think she finally accepted it, but your explanation as to how the confusion arose would help."

Hmm, some backpedaling required with Susan Warrington tomorrow, Sabrina feared. "Susan will be pleased to hear," she said, "that I'm willing to support you publicly in the race for governor."

He stilled. "Is this in exchange for me supporting your school?" His hand went to his back pocket, as if he might write a check this instant.

"That…and more." She finished the glass of wine. "You have to be my fiancé. Not my real fiancé," she hastened to add. "And not forever. Just until I'm settled in my new job."

Something dawned in his eyes, and it wasn't gratitude. "The new job you got all by yourself, the one that proves you're finally grown-up and independent?"

She swallowed, and wished someone would hurry up and invent the self-replenishing wineglass. "There's been a glitch. A temporary one. My recent media exposure damaged my credibility as a spokesperson for the trust."

He snorted. "The Miss U.S.A. garbage?"

"The trust—the directors—said I lack gravitas."

"Well, you do."

"Thank you so much," she hissed, seeing a chance to reclaim the moral high ground. For good measure, she let her lower lip quiver, a tactic she'd been known to employ in her younger days, but one she wouldn't have resorted to now in anything but the direst emergency.

The quivering bypassed Jake. "Sabrina, you've never been serious in your life." He paused. "Except when you were learning to walk again. You were damn serious about that."

"That's how I feel about this job," she said urgently. "It's that important. All I need to convince these people I'm more than a pretty face is you as my fiancé—"

"Let's get this straight," he interrupted. "You actually told this Richard Ainsley we're engaged? It's not some wrong conclusion he jumped to?"

This was it. She closed her eyes, and jumped. "Yes."

She peeked through her lashes as he flung a wild glance around the room. When he turned back, his eyebrows were a dark, angry slash. "But it's a lie. A crazy lie."

"I only told Richard. And the other members of the Trust's board. I said it's a secret, but obviously—"

"You lied."

Did he have to keep stating the obvious? Several people were looking at them. Sabrina leaned into Jake, trying to signal the need for discretion.

"Think about it, Jake, this could be good for both of us. Getting engaged is far better than my endorsement of your campaign. You said yourself I'm more popular than ever thanks to my legs."

"You would *marry* me to get this job," he said, dazed.

"Technically, no. But it will appear that we're getting married."

He clutched his head. "You're sabotaging my campaign."

"I'm *saving* your campaign. In the past few weeks, the newspapers have speculated that you're having an affair with a married woman, that you're dating a coed, that you're secretly engaged to the daughter of a former Indian prime minister."

"None of that's true," he snapped.

"Now people will know for sure."

There was a charged silence while he absorbed her logic.

"All you have to do is say yes to my proposal." Bad choice of words; Sabrina winced. "Proposition," she amended.

He rubbed his temples. "This is the kind of idea only you could come up with. Breaking up with you was like breaking out of Fairyland."

Her eyes smarted, but she said airily, "And I'll bet you miss the magic."

He held her gaze, staring her down for several long seconds. Long enough for Sabrina to regroup. She grabbed his arm, determined to make her point before he stormed out and denounced her to Richard Ainsley. "I'm sure you have interns hitting on you all the time—" she swallowed her pride "—just like I used to."

He scowled as he looked down at her hand on his arm. "*I* hit on *you*." He shook his head, as if he couldn't believe he'd been so lacking in discrimination. "What's it to you if I encounter the occasional pushy intern?"

She stored away his admission that he'd pursued her,

and the precious shred of dignity it afforded. "An engagement will protect you from the single women who could wreck your campaign by misreading something you say or do."

"And all I have to do is change my education policy for the sake of your job," he said calmly. He'd never sounded more dangerous.

Sabrina lifted her empty wineglass to her lips, a fragile barrier. "It's not a change," she said. "It's a detail. You put special-needs education on the agenda, I'll do the rest."

"You're overlooking one small fact," he said. "Namely, you're the last woman on earth I would marry."

Ouch! Sabrina pressed a hand to her chest, stared at him. Desperation demanded she get over the insult. "Jake, your campaign is all about educational opportunities for everyone. You're deeply committed to young people and their learning, I saw it on your Web site."

"You visited my Web site?" Beneath his anger she discerned satisfaction that the last woman on earth that he would marry was interested enough to check him out online.

"By accident," she said. "I was running a Google search for *jerks.*"

Before he could stop himself, Jake barked a laugh. Naturally, Sabrina pounced on the brief cessation of hostilities. "Supporting my school isn't a big stretch, Jake." She turned cajoling, the way she used to when they were dating. Using that voice, she'd talked him into drinking the vile blue cocktail she favored at the time. And skinnydipping in the pool at the governor's mansion.

Silly things. Games. Nothing like this.

"You're insane," he said.

Or was *he?* Because much as he tried to fight it, she was starting to make sense. It was difficult to campaign as a bachelor—there was always the risk that a kiss on the cheek, an inadvertent touch, would be taken the wrong way. Susan often said her job would be easier if he had a girlfriend.

"Why does it have to be an engagement?" he asked. "Why can't we tell people we're dating?"

Her eyes widened, brightened. But when she spoke she was calm, pragmatic. Qualities Jake admired. Qualities about as far from Sabrina's nature as Mars was from Venus.

"We've been there, done that, five years ago," she said. "To be taken seriously, we need a commitment this time around. Anyway, I've already said we're engaged."

He tried to corral more arguments, but they eluded him.

"I'll let you think about it." She turned her back on him to study one of the paintings on the wall just beyond the cordon.

The square canvas was painted almost entirely black, with a thin gold line down the middle. Jake read the caption over her shoulder: Inside The Elevator During a Power Cut.

Sabrina started to giggle; there was an edge of hysteria to it.

"This picture sums up how I feel," Jake said grimly.

"In the dark?" Her voice wobbled.

"Trapped." He shoved his hands in his pockets. "This isn't funny, Sabrina." Because no matter that she was letting him *think about it,* he didn't have a choice. She'd told people they were engaged, there was no way such juicy news wouldn't spread, even if she rescinded it. The press would be onto it; Jake would have to publicly contradict a woman often described as "Georgia's darling." More damage to his reputation, his campaign.

She must have read his thoughts. "It's really not that complicated. We'll say we're engaged, my appointment will be confirmed, then I'll endorse your campaign and attend a few events with you. As many as you want. Jake, this is exactly what you wanted, only…different."

Sabrina, the ultimate optimist—it must have taken a lunatic sense of optimism to persevere the way she had after the accident.

"This is the only way you'll get my support," she said.

The only way he could win.

"If you win the primary," she continued, "I'll stick with the engagement until the election in November."

Hell, it was bad enough pretending to be her fiancé for the six weeks until the primary. November was seven months away. "Why should I trust you, when you've never stuck with anything else?"

"Because this time," she said, "I'm claiming dumping rights."

"You're claiming *what?*"

She flashed a smile at the wait-kid who offered a tray of cheese puffs over the cordon and waved him away.

"One of us has to dump the other," she told Jake. "As soon we're through the election, I'll dump you."

He wished he'd accepted that drink the principal had offered. "Why wouldn't we announce we separated by mutual agreement?"

"Everyone knows that's a line put out to save face, and that someone did the dumping."

"Why should it be you?"

"It's my turn," she said reasonably.

"Fine," he said. "You get to dump me." The trapped-in-the-elevator painting loomed in his peripheral vision. "Just so long as you do get around to it. I don't care if you could make me president of the United States, I am *not* going to marry you. Got it?"

"Loud and clear." She tossed her blond hair, but somehow it didn't muss. "And don't you get any ideas about groping me when we have to kiss in public."

Kiss in public? His lips tightened. "There isn't a chance in hell that I'll grope you."

"Really? Because you used to have trouble keeping your hands to yourself."

She was right, dammit. Back then, she could shred his self-control with just a wiggle of her hips.

"Trust me, it won't be a problem." He meant it…and yet he couldn't help looking at Sabrina's mouth, thinking about those public kisses they'd be expected to share. Her lips were a perfect pink bow, temptingly plump at the bottom. What the hell was he thinking, buying into her scheme?

Jake looked at her with such loathing, Sabrina

flinched. She was used to getting her way through coaxing and flirting. Here, she was an amateur trying to play hardball with a professional. She needed to stop antagonizing him, or he would never agree, she would lose her job and she'd be back at square one.

"Sabrina, Baby." Her father's hearty voice, booming the childhood nickname, reached her before he did, giving her a chance to compose a relaxed smile. Jonah Merritt removed the cordon so he could pull her into a bear hug, squashing her against the plaid sports jacket that for him counted as casual clothing. "Sweetheart, I figured out how we're going to sue those guys." He jerked a thumb in the direction of the art critic from the *Atlanta Journal-Constitution,* whose ultrahighbrow reputation meant he refused to take an interest in a beauty queen. "They don't get to say your thighs are chunky without paying you a lot of money."

"Dad, stop," she said, alarmed. Who would believe her father was one of Atlanta's top lawyers, when he sounded like an ambulance chaser? "I don't want to sue them."

"It's libel, and we can prove it."

She folded her arms and glared at him, relieved to have an excuse to ignore Jake's glower. "Will proving it involve close-up shots of my thighs, measurement of my body-fat content and expert testimony?" She might not have attended law school, but she knew how lawsuits worked.

Her father must have picked up on the warning in her tone, because he said with uncharacteristic vagueness, "Well, uh, that sort of technical evidence is generally welcome in cases of this nature."

"Dad, my legs are not technical evidence. I'm not suing anyone, I just want to get on with my life."

Unaware he was first on the list of people who would soon have to butt out of her affairs, her father beamed. "That's very generous of you, sweetheart."

Jake made a gagging sound.

"Jake, good to see you." Jonah clapped him on the shoulder. Sabrina's father thought Jake was the best thing since the First Amendment. The two men shook hands, both strong, tough and self-controlled. For both, reputation meant everything. It occurred to Sabrina belatedly that her father would be horrified at her faking an engagement. Jake was right, this was a bad idea. She could tell the trust they were dating, as he'd suggested, and that in her excitement she'd jumped the gun on the engagement...

"Glad you're running for governor," Jonah said. "That takes guts in your situation. You've got my vote."

"Pleased to hear it." Jake's voice was strained. "There's something else I'd like from you, Jonah."

"I told Susan I'd be happy to donate. My checkbook's at home, but I can—"

"No." Jake spoke sharply. Then he smiled. A tighter effort than his vote-winning smile, one that didn't engage his eyes. "I want to ask for Sabrina's hand in marriage."

CHAPTER FOUR

"I SHOULD SLAP YOU both silly for not telling me this was going on." Susan Warrington tried to sound severe, but wasn't this exactly what she'd wanted for Jake? For him to find the happiness he sorely needed? She couldn't keep the smile from her voice.

She couldn't let them off scot-free, either. This campaign had enough problems to turn the rest of her hair gray, without secrets popping up out of the woodwork. She eyed Jake and Sabrina across the battered, lacquered table that took up most of the meeting room at Jake's campaign headquarters and drummed her fingers, waiting.

"I'm sorry, it's all my fault," Sabrina said, immediately contrite. The poor girl looked half-asleep; she'd had a horrible few days. But now she had Jake to look after her.

"Sorry, Aunt Sue." Jake usually called her Susan; she read his reminder of the family connection as an attempt to butter her up.

Ah, well, it was working. She loved Jake almost like a son, and the news that he and Sabrina were getting married was…simply wonderful. And not just from a political perspective.

"We weren't planning to tell anyone other than Sabrina's dad just yet," Jake continued. "But Jonah made a public announcement in the middle of the Wellesley art show."

"Who would have thought the *Journal-Constitution*'s art critic had the gumption to recognize a news story when it hit him in the face?" Susan unfolded the newspaper she'd brought from home. A photo of Jake and Sabrina dominated the top half of the front page.

Jake leaned forward in his swivel chair; it creaked ominously. Just yesterday Susan had been thankful he hadn't invested in any fancy furniture for his campaign office. Now it looked as if they might have a chance, after all. Jake read the headline, and snorted a laugh.

"Oh, dear," Susan said. "I assumed you'd seen this."

Sabrina picked up on her alarm and roused herself. She pulled the newspaper toward her. The headline beneath the photo screamed, Jake and Sabrina: Diamond Despite Dimples.

"How dare they?" Sabrina sputtered. "My thighs do not have dimples."

"So sue them," Jake said irritably. "You don't have a diamond, either."

"I know you two are used to, um, bantering with each other," Susan said, bemused. "But other people might mistake that *familiarity* for hostility. Jake, darling, you should be a little more conscious of how you speak to our sweet Sabrina."

Better to be a man with a few rough edges than one who appeared quiet and honest, but who would stoop to taking a bribe.

"We'll soon fix the lack of a ring," Susan said quickly, refusing to let thoughts of Ted Warrington ruin this special day. "Paul Kadowski, you'll remember him, Jake, the Warringtons have bought rings from him for generations, will be arriving—" she glanced at her slim gold-and-diamond watch "—any minute."

Jake's hand covered his wallet, on the table next to his cell phone. "There's no rush, is there?"

Typical man. He evidently didn't notice his fiancée's wistful gaze at her bare fingers.

"Of course there's a rush," Susan scolded him. "You want everyone to know Sabrina's yours, don't you?"

"I, uh—"

He looked adorable, with that flush along his jaw line. If the voters could see him now...

"Besides," Susan said, "you'll need the ring for the photos. I've scheduled a photo shoot for nine o'clock. We'll do it in my garden, it's a lovely morning."

"Photos?" Sabrina put a hand to her cheek.

"Official engagement portraits," Susan said. "We'll hold a press conference this afternoon." It wasn't even 7:00 a.m. yet, but calls were flooding in from the media. She'd arranged for a couple of interns to come in early to work the phones. The blinds remained closed in this room so no one could point a camera lens at them through the window.

"No press conference," Jake said.

"Jake, dear, this is the best news your campaign has had since we started." After having run Ted Warrington's campaign with such sure instincts, Susan felt as if she was wandering in a fog with Jake's. He'd insisted she take the job, insisted they both needed to do this to expunge the past. And he was probably right. But she'd lost faith in her own judgment, thanks to Ted, and with it her winning edge.

"Our engagement is our private business," Jake said. "I'm happy to release a statement and some official photos, but if the media want more, they'll have to pay attention to my campaign."

One thing about Ted, he'd been willing to listen to advice. When Jake got an idea in his head, he wouldn't be moved. Susan sighed. "Luckily, the reporters will be interested enough to play it your way. We can position the news in a positive light, that you're not exploiting your engagement for the publicity."

Jake winced; Sabrina pursed her lips.

Worry niggled at Susan. "Neither of you is radiating newly engaged joy right now. Is there a problem?"

"Sorry, Aunt Sue," Jake said. "I guess neither of us got much sleep last night."

She held up a hand. "Too much information." She tapped her pen against her notepad. "We'll release a statement with enough detail that the public gets the romantic picture." She turned to Sabrina. "Now, don't think I'm being nosy, dear, but I must ask...are there any complications that might pose a risk to Jake's campaign?"

Sabrina's eyes met Jake's.

"Any jealous ex-boyfriends?" Susan prompted her. "These days young people seem to have a predilection for videoing—" she cleared her throat delicately "—all kinds of things."

"I haven't dated in a while," Sabrina said. "And there are no home movies." Her cheeks were pink.

"Of course not." Susan patted her hand. "Have you two set a wedding date?"

"Not before the election," Jake cut in.

"A wedding would do wonders for your polling..." She trailed off into suggestion.

"No," Jake said sharply. He added, "We don't want to rush into marriage for political reasons. This engagement is enough to help my campaign, right?"

"Of course." Susan clasped her hands. "Voters are going to lap you two up. Maybe we could do a photo shoot for *Southern Woman* magazine—*Jake and Sabrina at home.* People can see where you have breakfast in the mornings, where you cozy up to watch TV at nights, that kind of thing."

Jake recoiled. "The only thing less appealing would be a slow-mo movie of someone flossing their teeth," he said. "Even that's a close call."

Susan couldn't help laughing. "Seriously, Jake..."

"We're not living together," Sabrina said. "Can the magazine wait until after the wedding?"

Susan sighed. "I suppose so. Are you sure you won't move in with Jake? For security reasons? I'm sure we can square it with voters." Jake's expression hardened. "Okay, okay." She scanned the notes she'd made so far for the media statement. "You know, Jake, even if Sabrina wasn't the one person who can get the situation with your father off your back…" Her face felt tight, as it always did at the mention of her brother-in-law. Consciously, she relaxed into a smile. "Well, you'd still be the luckiest man in Atlanta."

"Thanks, Susan." Sabrina smiled sleepily.

Susan stood. "I'll go get started on this statement. I'll have one of the interns send the jeweler in when he arrives."

As soon as Susan left, Sabrina dropped her head onto her arms, folded on the table and groaned.

Jake scowled at her. She'd be a hell of a lot more useful to his campaign awake. He poured her another coffee, slid the cup toward her. It sloshed over the side. He slapped a paper napkin over the spill. "Drink this," he said, "and wake up. You'll never survive the campaign trail if you can't get up at six-thirty. The early bird catches the worm."

"I'm a beauty queen," she said. "I need my *beauty* sleep."

He wished he could agree, but there wasn't a damn thing wrong with her appearance, even without makeup. He realized he'd never seen her like this. When they'd dated, she'd somehow always managed to have her makeup on by the time he saw her in the morning.

Now, the slight heaviness of her eyelids gave her a sultry look—it was an unsettling change from fresh-faced-and-deceptively-innocent.

"Lying to Susan felt awful," she said. "I didn't think about all the implications of saying we're engaged."

He rolled his eyes. "And you're usually so careful to think before you blab."

"Jewelers, photographers, questions about sex videos..." She pressed her palms to her cheeks.

"Were you lying about that, too?" His stomach tightened at the thought of Sabrina and some jerk—

"Of course not."

His tension eased, but not much. "What happened to that accountant you were dating?" Jake asked.

"We broke up three months ago."

"Let me guess." He pushed his chair away from the table, away from her. "He wasn't romantic enough?" It was a complaint she'd made about Jake.

"Chas was as overprotective as Dad," she said. "Which is probably why Dad introduced us."

"Weren't you seeing an IT consultant, too?"

She sighed. "Nice guy, but with a tendency not to let me out of his sight."

Jake hissed his disgust.

"You seem to know a lot about my dates," she countered.

"For some reason, people like to keep me informed."

"How about you?" she asked. "You were seeing that lobbyist...Tammy?"

Tammy had been the latest in a long line of women he'd dated since he broke up with Sabrina. He hadn't let himself get as entangled with anyone as he had with her.

"That's over," he said shortly.

Of course, because he didn't want to talk about it, Sabrina did. "Who ended it, and why?"

"None of your business."

"I need to know, Jake," she said sensibly. "Tammy has plenty of friends in political circles, people will think it odd if I don't know your history."

Annoyingly, she was right. "She was getting too serious," he muttered.

Sabrina cupped her ear. "I'm sorry, I didn't hear that."

He shot her a look of intense dislike. "She was talking marriage, okay?"

"And she seemed such a smart woman," Sabrina marveled. "Who'd have thought she'd make such a basic error?"

He paced to the window, but there was no escape there.

"After our engagement's over," she said, "send your girlfriends to me and I'll fill them in on how not to make fools of themselves over you." She clamped a hand over her mouth, as if that hadn't come out as planned.

Intrigued, Jake returned to the table and leaned on the back of his chair. "You think you made a fool of yourself over me?"

"I was an idiot," she said.

"That lends credence to my theory that you set up my dad for those pajama pictures because you were mad at me."

She sucked in a breath that reminded Jake of a dragon preparing to breathe fire. Except Sabrina had never breathed fire in her life.

Before she could attempt any incineration, there was a tap on the door. The jeweler, Paul Kadowski, entered. "Good morning, good morning."

Kadowski had sparse gray hair and the refined air of a man who spent his days surrounded by exquisite gems. The heavy, locked briefcase he carried proved to hold two velvet-wrapped trays of engagement rings. He set them on the shabby table with an air of reverence. "May I congratulate you on your engagement," he said, "and invite you to choose a symbol of your unity."

A fake rock would be the most appropriate symbol, Jake thought. But Sabrina bent over the rings with all seriousness.

Jake watched her appraisal...and saw the moment she made her choice. She straightened in her chair, darted a still-smoldering look at him.

"Which one?" he asked, resigned.

She pointed. The ring wasn't the biggest on the tray—though the diamond was respectably large—but something about the stone's cut and clarity, the way it sparkled, made it stand out.

"Ah, the elegant oval cut—an excellent choice," Paul Kadowski said. Which Jake figured meant it was expensive. But he'd already resolved to consider the ring an investment in his campaign.

"We'll take it," he said.

There was a moment of awkwardness where nobody moved.

"Jake, *darling,*" Sabrina said, "you need to put it on my finger."

With Kadowski watching, Jake gritted his teeth and picked up the ring. Sabrina extended her left hand. Her nails were painted a light purple. Of course they were. Other women, sensible women, would choose pink or red, but Sabrina had to do everything her own whimsical way.

Jake slid the ring over her knuckle. She trailed her fingers up to his wrist. "Thank you, darling."

A current of unexpected, infuriating desire surged through him; he blanked his expression while he freed his hand.

"Perhaps a little loose," Kadowski murmured. "See how it feels for a day or two, my dear, and consider having it adjusted."

When he'd packed up his rings and gone, Sabrina held her finger up so the diamond caught the light. "To think five years ago I would have fainted for joy if you'd put a ring on my finger."

Was she trying to provoke the argument the jeweler's arrival had interrupted? "You were way too young to be thinking like that."

"Twenty-one isn't too young."

"You'd only been out of high school for a year."

Because of the accident, she'd graduated late. She'd completed just one semester at Georgia State—Jonah hadn't wanted her to go away to college, Jake recalled—when she started as an intern in Jake's father's office.

"I know how I felt, Jake," she said. "I cared far too much to... I would never have acted against you or your father out of spite."

Ah, so she *was* referring to his earlier comment. If Jake

responded now, they'd be fighting so bitterly that no one would believe they were engaged. "You were right about not visiting the past," he said. "Let's look ahead."

"That photo shoot," Sabrina said. "I need to get changed and put on makeup."

His eyes skimmed the apricot sweater that hugged her curves. "If you say so."

She kept him waiting nearly an hour at her father's house before she emerged, wearing cropped pants that showed off her slim ankles and a dark blue, lacy top that revealed a flash of midriff when she moved. Some men might have considered that sliver of midriff worth the wait, Jake supposed.

Susan's home was just a couple of minutes away. Chris Martin, the photographer, was waiting outside. After keying in the security code to open the gate, Jake showed the guy around the half acre of immaculate gardens that rivaled Susan's sons in her affections.

They settled on two locations: the hothouse that was home to Susan's precious orchids and the swimming-pool complex.

Sabrina, of course, was a natural in front of the camera. The photographer took several shots of her on her own among the orchids, showing off the ring, as delighted as if she'd truly become engaged.

It was uncomfortably warm in the hothouse; the sweet, almost fruity scent of the flowers hung heavy in the air. Jake ran a hand across the back of his neck and eyed the water that trickled invitingly over black rocks into a small pond.

Behind him, a light flashed. "Over here, Jake," Chris called. "I'll get some shots of you on your own, then we'll put the two of you together."

Jake handed his jacket to Sabrina to hold, and let the guy do his worst. Within half a minute, he heard the buzz of his cell phone and made an instinctive move toward it.

"Stay where you are," the photographer warned. "That sun's just right."

"I'll get it." Sabrina rummaged in Jake's jacket, and before he could tell her not to, she'd pulled out his phone.

She pressed to answer. "Jake Warrington's phone."

Silence greeted Sabrina.

"Hello?" she said again. "I hear breathing," she told Jake.

The quality of the silence changed. She read the phone display—the call had ended. "They hung up. Do you have any stalkers?"

"Not as many as you, I'm sure." Jake turned his head to the left at the photographer's request, giving Sabrina a view of his profile. He was too handsome for his own good.

"Stalkers don't go for fat-thighed chicks," she said.

His mouth tensed, as if to guard against an inadvertent smile.

"Maybe it was Tammy," she speculated.

"It wasn't Tammy." He frowned, and the photographer uttered a mild curse.

"How do you know? It's not long since you broke up, is it?"

"A couple of months," Jake admitted with obvious reluctance.

"Was she upset?"

An exasperated look. "Maybe a little."

"Poor woman."

"Surely you think she's better off without me."

"Absolutely." Sabrina realized Chris had stopped shooting and was eyeing them with perplexity. "Don't mind us," she said.

He shrugged, and began looking through the photos he'd taken so far.

Jake came over and held out a hand for his phone. Sabrina whisked it behind her back.

"*I* know she's better off without you, but does Tammy know that?" she asked. "Or is she, right now, alone in her apartment, sobbing at the news you're engaged? You probably said something when you dumped her, like, 'It's not you, I'm just not ready for commitment.'"

When Jake reddened, she felt a stab of triumph.

"It's none of your damn business," he growled, low enough that Chris wouldn't hear.

"So by getting engaged to me," she continued, "you might as well have called her up and said, 'It *was* you, you were the problem.'"

"She wasn't," Jake protested. "And I'm *not* ready for commitment. This engagement is a sham."

"But she doesn't know that." Sabrina bit her lip; she'd been where Tammy was now, and she knew how it felt. "Maybe you should call her."

"And say what? 'It really *wasn't* you'?"

"There's no need to snap." She weighed the phone

in her hand. "I'm just thinking, if she's upset enough to call you the moment we announce our engagement…"

"You have no idea if that was her." He reached around her to grab his cell. His chest bumped against hers, startling her into releasing the phone. Jake checked caller ID. "Number withheld," he muttered.

"You see." Sabrina grimaced. "Poor Tammy."

He looked as if he wanted to hold her head under the fountain and not let go. "Let's get this straight. You're my fiancée and you feel sorry for my ex-girlfriend. It reminds me of the time you had bacon for breakfast, then sobbed all the way through my father's official visit to a pig farm."

"That was in my semivegetarian phase." She held up a hand. "And before you go accusing me of not sticking with it, all girls go through that phase, I was just a little later than most."

He zipped his lips in conspicuous self-restraint.

"And it's rude to liken Tammy to a pig."

"I didn't—"

"When I suspect she's hurting," Sabrina finished.

"Okay, guys, I'm ready for you both now." Chris pointed. "Sabrina, I want you next to these pink flowers. Jake, stand behind your fiancée with your arms around her waist."

Jake stepped up behind Sabrina. Gingerly, he put his arms around her—if she made any cracks about Tammy or about groping… She quivered as his hands rested on her abdomen. She felt slight, yet substantial, warm but distant.

Chris examined the camera's display. "Closer, Jake."

Jake tightened his hold.

"Lean into him, Sabrina."

She hesitated, then adjusted her stance so her back was against Jake's chest. He caught the tropical, coconut scent of her hair. The lacy fabric of her top seemed too thin, providing no protection between him and her flesh. Over her shoulder, he could see the swell of her breasts below her scooped neckline.

"Smiles." The photographer sounded sharp, as if he shouldn't have to tell two media-savvy people how to perform for the camera.

They both smiled to his satisfaction and he took a couple of shots. "Now, facing each other, holding hands."

Jake assumed it would be easier not having his arms around Sabrina. But standing eye-to-eye with her, closer than he'd been in years, he could see flecks of violet in her irises. Dropping his gaze took him straight to the bow of her mouth. It made him...hungry.

Sabrina's gaze met his and she licked her lips.

"Are we done yet?" Jake shifted his weight from one foot to the other. "I haven't had breakfast."

The photographer snapped away. "Just one more," he said cheerfully.

Anything, so long as this could end soon.

"A kiss," Chris announced.

Sabrina's gaze flew to Jake's.

"The first of many public displays of affection, *darling*," he said.

She lifted her chin. And puckered up.

Some primitive instinct triggered within Jake; blood rushed to his head. Before he could think it through, he leaned in and kissed her. Her lips were sweet temptation. They enticed him, and even though the kiss was strictly a tame, closed-mouth affair, he couldn't pull away.

Sabrina had resolved she would fasten her lips to Jake's for as long as it took for Chris to get his shot. The kiss would be devoid of feeling.

But her response to the touch of Jake's mouth was instinctive. No matter that she hadn't kissed him in five years, her mouth still knew exactly how best to fit against his. *When Jake kisses me, I kiss back.* His lips were the same, but different, their contour unchanged, but somehow firmer as he explored her mouth with a questing hunger she recognized. How would it feel to open for him, to allow the glide of—

"That's great, guys," the photographer said, with a laugh in his voice that said her reaction hadn't gone unnoticed. "I wish all engaged couples were as good looking as you two."

Better to be in love than good looking.

Jake released her—when had his hand gone to her nape?—and took an abrupt step backward. The sense of abandonment that overtook Sabrina was all the sharper for its unexpectedness.

No. I don't want *Jake, not after all these years.* She turned away, desperate to avoid his eyes, and in her confusion picked one of Susan's prize blooms. With trembling fingers she tucked it into her hair. Too late to put it back now.

CHAPTER FIVE

SABRINA'S FIRST OPPORTUNITY to publicly support Jake came two days after the photo shoot. He was scheduled to participate in a TV debate with one of the other candidates for governor.

Jake handed her a folded piece of paper as she got into his car. "Read this."

"More terrible poll results?" She opened it because it postponed, just a little longer, having to look him in the eye for the first time since that embarrassing kiss. No numbers or statistics on the page, just some kind of speech.

"When people ask you about me," he said as he pulled out of her father's driveway, "this is what you should say."

"'Jake's policies are farsighted, reflecting his vision for our state,'" she read aloud. "Ugh." She dropped the note as if it was contaminated.

Jake's eyes followed its fluttering journey to the floor of the car. "Pick that up," he ordered.

"Watch the road," Sabrina ordered back. "Jake, that PR pap isn't the kind of thing I would say."

"I'm trying to get you to say the *right* thing," he retorted.

"If it doesn't sound like me, it won't be the right thing."

He groaned as he pulled up to a red light. "Can't you just do as I ask?"

"Fine." Sabrina retrieved the speech he'd written for her. She pulled a pen from her purse. "After I make a few changes."

"Sabrina, this is important. It's my first debate. I don't want to be worrying about your loose lips."

Which made her think about that kiss. She ignored him, and began crossing out most of his words. She was determined to keep her side of their bargain, and that meant endorsing Jake to the best of her ability. It did not include reading out some bland PR blurb.

Halfway to the TV studio, Jake's cell phone rang. He reached into the storage tray below the stereo for it. But Sabrina was faster. Their hands tangled briefly; she grabbed the phone.

"I'll take it," Jake said.

"Not while you're driving. It's not safe."

He must have recognized the anxiety in her voice and remembered her aversion to risky-driving behaviors, because he didn't argue. No caller name showed on the phone's display. "Jake Warrington's phone."

No answer.

"Hello?" Sabrina said.

Silence. "Tammy, is that you?"

Still, no one spoke. Apart from Jake, who muttered a curse.

"Tammy, please, don't be upset…" Static crackled. Sabrina read the display. "She hung up."

"You don't know it was her," he said.

Sabrina slipped the phone back into its compartment. "I have an instinct for these things."

Jake snorted.

They arrived at the TV station with ten minutes to spare. A couple of schoolgirls stood outside, wrapped in scarves and hats against the morning chill. When they saw Jake's car, they waved the placard they were holding. The bright red letters read Sabrina Is Cool and Skinny.

"How much are you paying them?" Jake asked.

She smacked his arm. "They must be from the high school I visited a couple of weeks ago, before Vegas. Aren't they sweet?" The girls' support was balm to her bruised ego.

"Adorable," Jake said. "Why were you visiting a high school?"

"It was a Miss Georgia thing. The school board asked me to give a talk in support of their abstinence program."

Jake choked. "*You're* advising schoolkids about sex?"

"Why not? I'm good at it." She paused. "The advising *and* the sex." Just in case he thought he was the only guy she kissed the way she'd kissed him the other day.

She smirked as Jake's hands tightened on the steering wheel.

"Could you think before you open your mouth today?" he said as he swung the car into the underground parking garage. "No surprise announcement of our wedding date, no accidental revelation that our engagement isn't real?"

"Get over it, Jake. Surely you can trust me that far."

He eased the car into a tight spot between two others, and didn't speak until he'd finished. "I *have* to trust you."

He sounded as if all his nightmares had come at once.

SABRINA AND SUSAN HAD front-row seats in the studio audience. Jake's opponent—a congressman with ten years, three kids and a devoted wife on Jake—was good, but Jake came across as both personable and very knowledgeable. Viewers in the studio voted him the winner by a narrow margin.

Sabrina cheered along with the rest of the crowd.

"The official winner won't be declared until tonight." Susan leaned over to explain. "The debate will screen at seven-thirty, and viewers at home will be invited to text their votes. But I think Jake's nailed it."

Marlene Black, the highly respected current-affairs presenter hosting the debate, began a wrap-up to the cameras. She touched on the other candidate's strong record in Congress, his blameless past. Then she moved on to Jake.

"Jake Warrington has struggled in the polls because of a perception he's untrustworthy. But earlier this week, he announced his engagement to Miss Georgia, Sabrina Merritt, the woman who blew the whistle on Jake's father, Governor Ted Warrington, when he took a bribe in office. The woman who ended Ted Warrington's political career."

Good grief, did she have to put it so dramatically? Sabrina realized the cameras had panned the audience and were now focused on her.

"Sabrina, come on up here," Marlene said, "and tell us if Jake Warrington is more trustworthy than his father."

What?

Susan nudged her. "Go on."

"Did you know this would happen?" Sabrina demanded under her breath, smiling for the cameras. The other woman shook her head. Surely Jake hadn't anticipated anything this extreme when he'd said, *When people ask you about me?*

She couldn't refuse, not without looking as if she was reluctant to endorse Jake. Sabrina pushed out of her seat and walked up the steps onto the stage.

She shook hands with Marlene, accepted Jake's light kiss on her lips. At Marlene's invitation, she sat next to him on the couch.

"Sabrina," the presenter repeated, "is Jake Warrington more trustworthy than his father, disgraced former governor Ted Warrington?"

This was it, the question their ruse was intended to answer. The question Jake didn't *trust* her to answer.

She was supposed to spout words about his sound, practical policies, making specific references to education and health care. Sabrina hesitated. Beside her, Jake tensed.

"Marlene, I would trust Jake with my life—" *if not my heart* "—and I trust him to run the state I love so much." Sabrina held the presenter's gaze; she knew to let the cameras find her, rather than create a shifty impression by glancing around. "If the people of Georgia want an honest man running this state, they should vote for Jake."

He grabbed her hand and squeezed, and the strength in his grip had a disconcerting effect on her insides.

"There you have it, folks." Marlene, arguably the most astute journalist in the nation, looked faintly skeptical. But it didn't come through in her voice. "Sabrina Merritt stands by her man."

The audience broke into loud applause that quickly escalated into foot-stamping and wolf whistles. Sabrina had noticed a high proportion of men in the crowd. A few guys near the front stood…then a few more…and next minute, Sabrina and Jake had a standing ovation.

Jake got to his feet to acknowledge the tribute, tugging Sabrina up with him. "Thanks," he murmured close to her ear through the din. "You were right. Thanks for being yourself."

Jake was willing to admit she was right? What the heck, she might as well seal the deal. Sabrina leaned in and kissed him on the mouth in front of the entire state.

Susan had invited Jake and Sabrina, along with most of their relatives, to watch the debate on TV at her place. They would have a meal beforehand, which would double as an engagement celebration.

Sabrina tried not to think about the lie they would be perpetrating on their families. Instead, she rehearsed her planned announcement of her new job ahead of the formal statement the trust would make tomorrow. She couldn't wait to see her father's and sisters' faces—they would understand just how perfect this opportunity was for her.

When she arrived with her father, Susan greeted her

with a hug. "Jake's here already, and so are Tyler and Bethany. Max will be late, he's still at the office, what a surprise." She shook her head. "I daresay your sisters will be late, too."

"Of course they will," Jonah said, proud that his oldest daughters could match Max's workaholism anytime.

He was even prouder when Max walked in barely a minute behind him and Sabrina. He clapped Max on the back as they all headed into the living room, where Jake was pouring champagne.

"Here comes the bride." Tyler rose from the couch and greeted Sabrina with a hug. "I was just saying to Jake, you guys have a nerve not telling us what was going on." He flashed the boyish grin that had captivated Atlanta's female population for years, until Tyler had fallen for the one woman who was impervious to his charms. Luckily, he'd managed to talk Bethany around. Sabrina could tell by the way he grabbed his wife's hand that he still couldn't get over his good luck.

Bethany disentangled herself long enough to give Sabrina a squeeze. She was considerably shorter than Sabrina, but so intense, it was only when she got this close that Sabrina noticed her height. "Yeah, what was that about?" Bethany demanded.

"What can I say?" Sabrina spread her hands. "Jake swept me off my feet." That provoked much teasing and hooting from everyone. Jake handed her a champagne flute; Sabrina kissed him briefly on the lips, ignoring the instant sizzle. She tapped her glass against his.

Tyler raised his glass, too. "Congratulations, guys, that's wonderful news. I always said if these two ever buried the hatchet they'd be in each other's arms, didn't I, Peaches?"

"He never said that," Bethany told them in resignation, and everyone laughed.

Tyler groaned. "Why didn't I marry a woman who would let me get away with something, *anything*, sometimes?"

"Because you'd get bored with her." Bethany hugged Sabrina again. "I'm so excited for you—and so excited that we'll be related."

Sabrina returned the embrace, without speaking. Tyler had been one of her closest friends for years, and she loved his wife almost as much. She couldn't believe these two would be fooled by her and Jake's charade. But it seemed they were so bedazzled by their own love, they swallowed it without question.

"Where's Ben?" She asked after the couple's adopted baby son to change the subject.

"Asleep upstairs," Tyler answered. "He didn't get much of a nap this afternoon. The poor guy's exhausted."

Sabrina chuckled, enjoying the release of tension. Tyler's transition from least-likely father to devoted dad still took some getting used to.

He swatted her good-naturedly. "Wait until you and Jake have kids—Jake will be a ball of mush."

An awkward moment ensued, which Max eased by kissing Sabrina's cheek. Though he shared the same dark hair as Jake and Tyler, he was taller than the other two; he radiated command. "I'm glad you two got back together," he said. "Jake needs you."

That promptly created another awkward moment. Jake frowned at his cousin, but Max just smiled.

Next to arrive were Cynthia and Megan. It was the first time Sabrina had seen her sisters—half sisters, to be precise, though none of them ever thought of their relationship that way—since she got back from Las Vegas. Was it only five days ago? She'd accepted their congratulations on the engagement over the phone, but of course, they weren't done yet.

"Baby!" Megan hugged Sabrina. "I'm so happy for you."

"Yeah, nice catch, Baby." Cynthia grinned at Jake.

Jake mouthed, *Baby?*

Sabrina realized how odd the nickname sounded. Megan was only a couple of years older than she was, Cynthia three years older again. But the girls, and Jonah, had called her Baby for as long as she could remember. Jake had pointed out how weird it was five years ago— it sounded even stranger now.

Mitzy, Susan's beloved Cavalier King Charles spaniel, dashed into the room, yapping deliriously, having broken free of her confinement somewhere. Sabrina watched as every man in the room ignored the animal. Not only was that shrill yap likely to turn into a nip toward anyone Susan showed affection, but the dog often responded to attention by peeing indiscriminately. Unfazed at the prospect, Susan made a fuss of her pet. Bethany patted the dog, too.

"You don't have to pretend to like that mutt now we're married, Peaches," Tyler said.

Bethany slapped his arm, but she giggled. Sabrina bent down to scratch Mitzy where she knew the dog loved it, on her shoulders. "Hello, you beautiful girl."

"Don't encourage that fleabag," Max teased. Sabrina carried right on petting Mitzy, much to Susan's pleasure.

Jake felt Tyler's scrutiny and pinned what he hoped was a loving expression on his face as he watched Sabrina. She had everyone in the room, except him, rolling over in submission to her charm, but she seemed oblivious. As he looked on, she jumped to her feet and offered to help Susan serve the chili.

Smiling, Susan waved Sabrina back down again, but let Bethany join her in the kitchen. Even ten years after the accident, folk seemed to worry about Sabrina taxing her strength. Jake had witnessed her accepting their assessment—in other words, dodging drudgery—time after time. If this education job of hers turned out to require real work, she'd be in for quite a shock.

Dinner was cheerful and noisy—hard for it to be otherwise with Jonah and his overachieving daughters, particularly Cynthia, always willing to voice an opinion. Max and Tyler had a friendly sibling rivalry going that required each of them to get their shots in on any subject, although Tyler made sure Bethany received her share of attention. Her quick, dry wit made everyone laugh. It all added up to familiar chaos.

Jake joined in sporadically, but more often found himself hanging back, watching. He loved Susan and her sons, being with them felt more like home than his parents' place had ever been. His dad had always been consumed by high-and-mighty ideals about social justice, and his mom...well, she'd been fond of Jake, but she wasn't one of those mothers who ever hung out at home. Without Susan and her late husband, Henry, who'd insisted Jake join Warrington Construction after the scandal, Jake would have been entirely alone. Without them, Atlanta wouldn't have given him the time of day five years ago. Now, he was torn between loving these people and hating that he owed them his respectability.

They moved to the dining room, where the nine of them fit comfortably around the enormous oak table. Jonah sat next to Sabrina, and Jake sat opposite, beside Megan. Megan was reserved, but he knew better than to take it personally. She was the most low-key of the Merritt sisters, understandable given she couldn't match Sabrina's beauty, and that Cynthia's hard-nosed approach to her career made the oldest Merritt girl a favorite with Jonah. Megan was smart and attractive in an understated way, with her honey-colored hair and slim figure, and she didn't call attention to herself.

Jake sensed Sabrina's curious gaze on him. He lifted his eyebrows at her, and she glanced away. She wasn't saying much, either, though people constantly directed their remarks to her, unconsciously seeking the approval of the most beautiful person in the room.

Jake felt a twinge of envy, when he thought how hard he had to work a room just to secure a few votes.

"How's the Alverson divorce going?" Max asked Megan, as he topped his second helping of chili with sour cream. Megan was representing the wife of the well-known couple, whose property-development firm was a client of Warrington Construction's, in their divorce. Many of the details had been published in the newspapers, and Megan confined her conversation to what was in the public domain.

"So, the husband's cheating on her but she can't prove it, right?" Max asked, summing up her comments.

Megan nodded as she rounded up a stray piece of tomato with her fork. "Not even the private detective could find anything."

"Maybe he's not cheating," Sabrina said.

Everyone gave her a kind look, and she laughed.

"You always like to think the best, don't you, Baby," Megan said tolerantly.

Sabrina shrugged. "Why not give the guy the benefit of the doubt?" She poured more red wine from the bottle in front of her, then offered it to Jake.

That was her philosophy of life, Jake realized. She doled out the benefit of the doubt on the slimmest of pretexts—to Tammy, to Mitzy. The only time he'd known her refuse to extend that benefit had been five years ago. To him. And his father. If she'd had more faith in Jake, believed his promise that he would deal with the bribe in a way that was honest and right, but which would give his father a chance to retain some dignity…

"Baby, you'd give a shark the benefit of the doubt while it gnawed on your leg," Megan teased.

Sabrina smiled, but it was a tense movement of her mouth.

"You're not a good judge of character, sweetheart," Jonah chided his daughter.

Maybe that was how Jonah justified his overprotectiveness toward her.

"You don't need a law degree to understand what makes people tick," Sabrina said shortly.

"I just meant you're too nice," Jonah, sitting next to her, protested.

Sabrina tightened her grip on her silverware.

Jonah ruffled her hair—she immediately pulled out a compact mirror and began patting it down, which made Jake smile even while it irritated him. He'd never known a woman who checked her reflection as often as Sabrina.

"A toast to the happy couple." Jonah raised his glass for what had to be the fifth time, and everyone else good-naturedly followed suit.

After dinner, they ate chocolate brownies in front of the TV as they watched the debate, followed by Sabrina's brief interview with Marlene. Everyone commended Jake on his performance. He guessed the reason they didn't congratulate Sabrina was that they assumed her words had come naturally about the man she loved, rather than their being an incredibly well-judged piece of theater. When they held the live-viewer vote at the end of the show, revealing the results after an ad break, Jake won by a clear margin.

As they rehashed the debate, Susan left the room to

take a phone call. In the lull that followed her departure, Sabrina spoke up.

"I have some news to share with you all." Susan already knew about her new job, so she didn't need to wait for the older woman. "I've been appointed spokesperson for the Injured Kids Education Trust." As she went on to outline what the trust was about, what her work would involve, she heard herself getting carried away by her passion. "Basically," she said, taking a deep breath, "it's my dream job, and they think I'm the best person for it." Okay, so that was outright boasting, but apart from Miss Georgia, she'd never been the best person for anything.

"That's wonderful, Baby," Megan enthused. "It's great that they didn't want a professional lobbyist."

"Or someone used to high-level government work," Cynthia chipped in. "Well done, Baby. And if this doesn't work out, there are lots of other charities looking for good people."

Sabrina didn't need Jake's frown from across the table to figure that her sisters' reactions didn't exactly reflect confidence in her. Megan and Cynthia would be horrified to know they sounded catty—they were just applying their ruthless analysis to the situation, undoubtedly with the aim of protecting Sabrina from disappointment. Still, their comments rankled.

"It *will* work out. I know I can do this, and do it better than anyone else," she said sharply.

"Of course you can." Jonah directed a warning look at the other two.

"And I don't need you to tell them that," Sabrina said to her father. At Jonah's crestfallen look, she patted his hand on the table. He had adored Sabrina's mom, his second wife, and after her death, he'd clung to Sabrina almost as much as she'd clung to him.

"Is this a full-time job?" Tyler asked.

Before Sabrina could reply, Susan hurried back into the room. "I have an announcement." Excitement brimmed over in her voice. "That phone call was from the research company I had polling right after the debate ended." She paused for effect. "Jake, seventy-three percent of people who saw the debate—and saw Sabrina saying her piece—said they trust you."

Sabrina gaped. It was almost a direct reversal of the last poll Jake had shown her.

"The trust factor for the whole population, including people who didn't see the show, was only forty-six percent," Susan said, "but that's a big increase on last time, which I suggest comes down to your engagement." She drew a breath. "Keep going like this, Jake dearest, and you'll be governor in November."

Everyone broke into excited discussion. From the armchair next to where she sat on the couch, Jake shot Sabrina an apologetic look that her news had been swallowed up by this latest development, then he dived right into the thick of it. Of course, her father and sisters never once questioned Jake's ability to be governor. No, it was only Sabrina they doubted. She'd bet even Jake wouldn't attribute his newfound success to her "crazy idea" that they should fake an engagement. Let alone come out in vocal support of the injured kids school. Sure, he'd said a few words about special-needs education in the debate, but dozens of projects came under that umbrella.

Resentment simmered beneath the smile she kept on her face as she helped herself to another brownie from the plate on the coffee table. Might as well give the thigh-watchers something to get excited about.

"That's right, Sabrina." Tyler grinned. "Eat your brownie now. When you're the governor's wife your every mouthful will be reported."

She choked on a crumb, and thumped her chest. "Are you kidding? No way on earth would I be dumb enough—" Just in time, she stopped. *To marry Jake.*

Everyone, from Jonah down to Mitzy, was staring at her. Sabrina realized her mouth was still open; she snapped it shut.

"Dumb enough to care what the media say about you," Jake inserted smoothly. There was a reason why he was the politician around here. He stood, pulled Sabrina to her feet with just the strength of his fingers around her wrist. He smiled down at her. Only she saw the menace in his eyes, the anger that she'd almost exposed their lie with a careless comment. "Darling, it's time we told everyone our news."

News? What news? Sabrina's heart thudded.

"Sabrina's moving in with me tomorrow," Jake said.

CHAPTER SIX

WHAT JAKE HAD SAID PRODUCED almost as much excitement as his victory in the debate. One voice rose above the chorus of questions.

"I won't allow it," Jonah declared. "It's too sudden."

Thanks, Dad. Sabrina smiled at her father, though she knew his concern was mostly selfish. He hated it when she lived away from the family home. She wanted to leave, but not to go to Jake's. What the heck was he thinking?

"Don't be a fuddy-duddy, Jonah," Susan admonished him. "They're in love, they're getting married."

"And you want us to do an at-home feature with *Southern Woman* magazine," Sabrina muttered.

"That's a wonderful idea," Susan said, unabashed.

"Jake, we talked about this," she said sweetly, desperately. "I told you, the voters won't approve of us living in sin. It's too risky."

Jake's lips brushed her ear. "Nice try, *darling.*"

Susan pooh-poohed that objection, too. "As long as you're engaged, dear, people will be fine with it. Look at Senator Joe Glass, he and his fiancée have been living together over a year."

"I'd like to do this the old-fashioned way," Sabrina protested.

Megan chortled. "Move in with him, Baby, and I'll write you an ironclad prenup."

Sabrina would never go into a marriage with a prenuptial agreement, and Megan knew it.

"Now's not the time for cold feet, darling," Jake said. "I want you with me."

She read in his cold, hard expression the true reason for his sudden pronouncement: he didn't trust her. She'd forced him into this engagement and just now she'd almost blurted out their secret, and those indiscretions outweighed the leap in his poll results and her performance at the TV station.

Sabrina's shoulders sagged. She rubbed her chest, where it felt as if that brownie crumb had set up house. What had she thought? That Jake might have learned to value her for her insights and abilities, where no one else did? Good grief, she was every bit as starry eyed as she'd been at twenty-one.

"Sabrina." His tone was rock hard. He wouldn't back down. He wanted her where he could make sure she didn't slip up.

Her dad flexed his fingers at his sides, the way he did when he was worried. Susan lifted her glasses and peered at Sabrina. Any more arguing, and Jake wouldn't need to worry about her blabbing, everyone would have guessed the truth.

Sabrina sighed. "Fine, I'll move in."

SABRINA HEARD JAKE leave early on the first morning she woke up in his house. Too early—a glance at the sleek, bullet-shaped clock on his guest-room nightstand told her it was only seven. With a muttered "Good riddance," she burrowed under the featherlight duvet and went back to sleep.

She rose at eight, a much more civilized hour, and brushed her hair in front of the full-length mirror. The guest room was simply but elegantly furnished, the bronze duvet cover contrasting with the thick caramel-colored carpet beneath her feet.

Sabrina headed to the kitchen, taking with her the document she'd stayed up late last night to prepare. She would read it through while she ate breakfast. It might distract her from her seething over Jake's coercion, forcing her into his house.

A pot of coffee sat on a warmer on the kitchen counter, fractionally improving her outlook on the day. Sabrina poured a cup and carried it into the walk-in pantry. She emerged, clutching a box of granola just as a phone rang. Jake had left his cell on the end of the counter.

Sabrina let it ring through to voice mail, but then it rang again immediately. Jake might be calling to check where his phone was. She picked up.

Not Jake. Once again, his silent caller.

"Tammy?" Sabrina asked. Jake's ex-girlfriend certainly was persistent.

Or not—the line went dead.

Jake should call the woman and let her get her feelings off her chest—hadn't he told Sabrina she should confront her problems?

The phone on the kitchen wall next to the fridge rang. Sabrina sighed as she crossed to answer it, saying into the phone, "Tammy, don't hang up. Sweetie, I'll do my best to get Jake to call you. Just don't do anything hasty." What if the woman was heartbroken to the point of hurting herself?

"Sabrina—" the voice was angry, familiar, male, definitely not Tammy "—whoever the hell Tammy is, your bleating must have sent her off the nearest bridge by now."

Sabrina spun around, knocking a fridge magnet and the electricity bill it held to the floor. She clutched the phone with both hands. *"Ted?"*

Jake's *father?*

"Does Jake ever answer his own phone these days?" Ted Warrington demanded. "Or are you his secretary, as well as his fiancée?"

"You mean, *you're* the one who's been calling?" Sabrina nudged the fridge magnet with her toe as she processed this development. Ted was the silent caller, not Tammy.

"I wouldn't have to keep calling, if Jake would pick up his own damn phone."

"Ted, where are you?" Jake had said he didn't know where his father lived.

"I'm in Florida, I—" He broke off with an impatient exclamation. "What the hell is Jake doing, marrying you?"

Sabrina froze. "He— I— We love each other," she blurted.

Ted snorted, the mannerism so similar to Jake's, it was spooky. "I didn't even know he was seeing you again." He obviously kept up with Jake's news somehow.

"A, uh, lot of people didn't," she said.

"Are you pregnant?"

Sabrina gasped. "Of course not."

The breathy sigh over the airwaves was one of relief. "Is Jake there?"

"He left his phone at home. I don't know where he is."

"When can I reach him?" A simple question loaded with pain, sorrow, loneliness.

She closed her eyes, remembering how much Ted had lost—not just his job, but his home, his wife, his son—and the part she'd played in it.

"You can try calling again—" she recalled the harsh lines of Jake's face when he spoke of his father "—but I'm pretty sure Jake won't talk to you." She clapped a hand to her mouth. "I didn't mean to sound so blunt, I'm sorry."

"You always had a knack for shock announcements," Ted said.

He was still angry with her, just like his son. But however much Jake resented Sabrina, he resented his father more. How could he trust her, trust anyone, when he was staggering under a ton of bitterness?

"Jake *should* talk to you," she mused aloud. "He won't be happy as long as he's hung up on the past. If you were here, if we could get you two in the same room together..."

"You're inviting me to Atlanta while Jake's trying to get elected? Whose side are you on?" Ted demanded. "Or are you plumb crazy?"

Huh, like father, like son when it came to casting aspersions on Sabrina's sanity. How touching. Then she realized what he'd said. "Of course I didn't invite you to town." She went hot and cold at the mere thought of Jake's reaction to such an invitation. "Obviously now isn't the time for reconciliation."

"When *is* the right time?" Ted asked. "When Jake loses the election and blames it on me, or when he wins and faces even greater public embarrassment if I show my face?"

Sabrina gulped. "Uh..."

"Don't trouble your head about it," Ted said. "I'll figure it out." He ended the call.

Sabrina was still staring at the phone in mounting trepidation when Jake came in from the garage.

She squawked, dropped the handset, fumbled to catch it again. "I thought you'd gone out." She clattered the phone back onto its base.

"For a run," he said.

Which would explain why he was wearing a T-shirt and shorts. Sabrina lifted her eyes from his muscular legs and found she was staring at his chest. She remembered exactly what that chest looked like without a shirt, felt like...

Jake's eyes ran over her shoulders—bare except for the straps of her short, pink satin nightdress, printed with dancing butterflies. He checked the railway station–style clock on the wall. "Did you only just get up?"

She poured granola into a bowl. "I can't get up early, I need—"

"Your beauty sleep," he finished for her. He looked her over again, then down at the granola. "Make yourself at home."

"*You* made me at home," she retorted. "Just say the word, and I'll leave."

His mouth firmed. "You're staying."

"Jake, this is stupid," she said. "I don't want to be here, you don't want me here. Okay, so I made a momentary slip the other night. But I recovered."

"*I* recovered," he said. "One more second of stunned silence and everyone would have figured out the truth. I can't risk you giving us away."

"I wouldn't have said a word if I hadn't been goaded," she grumbled. "I'm not Miss Incompetent."

Just thinking about how close they'd come to screwing up made Jake irritated again. "I can't believe you let your family talk to you the way they do."

"They don't mean to be rude."

"Calling you Baby, treating you as if you don't have a brain in your head."

Sabrina grimaced at the milk carton, then poured it into her bowl anyway. Jake didn't want to know if the milk had too much fat, or not enough, or whatever.

"Cynthia and Megan have always been Supergirl and Wonder Woman. Literally," she said. "When we were kids, we played this game where they flew in and rescued me from dastardly criminals who tied me to railroad tracks or strapped me to nuclear warheads."

"Charming." He grabbed a glass from the cupboard

and went to the sink for some water. "What would they have done if they *didn't* like you?"

"All I'm saying is, they've never grown out of seeing me as their baby sister. It's not uncommon." She hitched herself up onto a bar stool, and her nightdress hiked up her thighs.

No way could Jake think of her as any kind of baby.

She caught him looking at her legs and pointed one foot at him. "Do you think I should paint my toenails lilac to match my fingers, or would a neutral color lend more gravitas?"

The flipping sensation in Jake's stomach as he eyed her bare feet definitely wasn't neutral. "I'm not sure I ever got the toenail theory of gravitas." He dragged his gaze away. "People won't take you seriously until you take yourself seriously. This hang-up about your looks being your biggest strength—get over it. Call your family on their attitude."

"I don't like conflict."

"The beauty-queen obsession with world peace," he guessed.

She dug hard into her granola, scraping the spoon on the bottom of the bowl. "There's been enough bad stuff in my family—Dad's acrimonious divorce from his first wife, Mom's death, my accident. I like to stay positive."

Jake swigged his water. "That's fine, as long as no one's picking on you."

"I can look after myself." She picked a piece of dried banana off her spoon and set it on the edge of her bowl. "On the subject of conflict, I've been thinking."

"Careful," he warned.

She stuck out her tongue. "Until you get over the past, you're only going to hurt other people and yourself."

"For Pete's sake, I did *not* hurt Tammy. Has she called again?" Jake banged his glass down onto the counter. Tammy had been smart and pretty and he'd liked her…but he'd never once found himself lying awake in bed thinking about her mouth. The way he had last night, knowing Sabrina was in the room right across the hallway.

He should have stayed with Tammy…but he'd wanted to start his campaign without any encumbrances. Which was funny, if you were into sick irony. "Twice now you've suggested breaking up with me is a shattering occurrence," he said. "Are you drawing on your own experience?"

Sabrina's gaze dropped, but then she resumed eyeing him. "I was devastated when I broke up with Chas."

"That's not what you said the other day."

"I struggled to hide my pain. Like Tammy's doing now."

She was harping on about Tammy to rile him; Jake didn't for one second buy into her theory about his ex-girlfriend's distress. He jammed his empty glass in the dishwasher. "Tammy wasn't upset when we broke up." But suddenly, he wasn't so sure. Damn Sabrina, with her ready sympathy for others. She was a pain in the butt, making him feel guilty where there was no need to be. Probably.

She popped a spoonful of granola into her mouth and

chewed. "Funny you should assume I was talking about Tammy when I mentioned hurting other people, if your breakup was as easy as you suggest. But actually, I was talking about your dad."

Jake held up a hand to stop her, but she continued. "About how your inability to forgive him is crippling your life."

The words hit him like a punch to the solar plexus. When he regained his breath, he fought back. "Dammit, Sabrina, butt out of my life. Next thing you'll be suggesting some kind of cozy reunion."

Her spoon clattered to the floor. She slipped off her stool to get it. "I'm not suggesting any such thing." Her voice was muffled as she bent over, and when she straightened, the blood had rushed to her face.

"I don't want to hear another word about my father," Jake said.

She rinsed her spoon, then returned to her breakfast. "But—"

"Sabrina," he interrupted. "We're going to be living together for at least six weeks, maybe seven months. Let's try to, as you would say, avoid conflict."

"Fine by me." She discarded another piece of dried banana. What did she have against the stuff? "I'm all in favor of peace in the home."

It occurred to Jake that home was probably a good place to start working on world peace.

"Jake, you always tell me what you think, without worrying about hurting my feelings." She'd made one of her lightning-quick changes of subject.

"I guess," he said.

"Would you mind reading this?" Sabrina pushed a pile of typed pages across the island. "It's some background information about the school. I prepared it last night for the policy and finance people at the Department of Education. I don't know if it's any good, and I'm sure you'll give me an honest opinion."

About thirty pages, he estimated. She'd done all this last night?

"If you read it now," she wheedled. "I'll pour you some coffee."

She batted her beauty-queen lashes at him. He rolled his eyes. "I suppose in the interest of *peace in the home* I could read it."

"I'll make a fresh cup." Sabrina didn't let him see how pleased she was he'd acquiesced. *A very hot cup that'll take you a long time to drink.* She pottered in the kitchen, putting the kettle on to boil so she could refill the press, stacking her plate in the dishwasher, making his coffee. Jake ignored her. With his head bent over the document, she could see the nape of his neck. She remembered how she used to sneak up behind him when he worked late at night, and blow hot breaths there. How he would swivel in his chair and grab her, haul her into his lap…

Cut it out. This is way more important than some ancient crush. If Jake, who didn't like her and wanted to support her less than anyone she knew, bought into her arguments, then Sabrina was certain she could win over the education department.

As she set the fresh coffee beside him, she caught a whiff of clean male sweat and damp cotton. She peered over his shoulder—already he was up to the section where she gave her personal take on the social and mental impact of spinal injury on a teen's life.

He looked quite engrossed. Sabrina couldn't help preening.

Jake lifted his head and caught her at it; he frowned. *That's right, disapprove. That ought to be a total turn-off.* Only right now, the muscular-body-in-shorts-and-T-shirt factor was overriding the disapproval factor.

"Don't you need to go and put your face on?" His gaze drifted over her curves, down her legs, suggesting he wasn't thinking about her face.

"Nope, I'm not trying to impress you." At least, not with her face or her body. Hmm, she wanted to impress Jake Warrington with her mind. Maybe she should start with something easier, like walking on Mars.

On that dispiriting thought, she went to get dressed.

When she arrived back in the kitchen half an hour later, Jake had finished reading. She slipped into the chair next to his.

He sat back. "Took a long time to *not* put your face on."

"The natural look is a girl's biggest makeup challenge."

"Tough," he said with feigned sympathy.

"I can handle it." She tapped the document. "What do you think?"

"Did you write this yourself?"

Jerk! "I started it," she said, "but just as my brain began to hurt, a little green alien appeared in my room and did it all for me." She pressed a hand to her chest. "You can imagine my relief."

He ignored her wiseass quip. "You've done an excellent job."

She squinted at him—no sarcasm. "Um, thanks." A rebellious corner of her mind noted that his chin was unshaven, and speculated about how it would feel beneath her fingers, against her cheek. *For Pete's sake, he's taking me seriously and I'm thinking about his stubble.* "So, how about you announce your support for the school as part of your education policy?"

He pushed his chair back from the table. "I already talked about special-needs education during the debate."

"I mean, specifically, support the Injured Kids Education Trust school. Commit to getting it into the budget for full state funding if you're elected." She pulled the document toward her, straightened the edges. "It's a perfect fit with your policies."

"Where did this come from?" Jake asked.

"I'm going to be endorsing your campaign all over town, I'd like you to do more for the school."

He drained his now-cold coffee, and grimaced. "I've already kept my side of the bargain—I helped you get your job, and I put special-needs education on the electoral agenda."

"You like what I wrote," Sabrina said. "Why can't you do more? Apart from the obvious reason."

His eyes narrowed. "Enlighten me. What's the obvious reason?"

"You're so hurt by the past, you can't bring yourself to support me."

He growled as he stood up. "If you mean I can't bring myself to trust you, you're damn right."

He stalked out of the room. A minute later, Sabrina heard a shower running upstairs. *Not thinking about Jake in the shower.*

Not thinking about peace in the home, either.

Could there be two more utterly pointless fantasies?

CHAPTER SEVEN

SABRINA SPENT THE NEXT several days on Miss Georgia duties and working with the Injured Kids Education Trust. The Miss Georgia activity was time-consuming, but not arduous: a high school visit that had been scheduled long ago; a Scrabble afternoon in a retirement home; judging a church bake-off. Her work for the trust, though, was stimulating, exciting, all she'd hoped it would be.

She worked with Richard Ainsley to refine the document Jake had read, then created a PowerPoint presentation around it. They planned to present it to all the key influential players who would give them the time of day.

"It will help that the school has Jake's support," Richard said as they reviewed the final version of the presentation. "If he's paying attention, others have to think about it, too."

Sabrina made a noncommittal sound. She could hardly tell her boss that Jake considered he'd done more than enough for her. "Some of the media seem more interested in what brand of toothpaste Jake uses than his education policies."

Susan had convinced *Southern Woman* magazine to run a five-page at-home feature about Jake and Sabrina.

"They come to the house, ask where you have breakfast, what music you listen to, that kind of thing," Susan had said breezily. "I know it sounds ghastly, but, Jake, it's the biggest-selling women's magazine in the state."

The interview was scheduled for early in the second week of their cohabitation. The reporter, Kara Simons, did indeed seem fascinated by every trivial detail of their lives. No question was too obscure for her, from how Jake took his coffee, to Sabrina's favorite shade of lipstick. Then there were the details of how they met, their feelings about family, about kids, about everything.

Sabrina noticed that although Jake took every opportunity to link his answers to his gubernatorial aspirations, his growing impatience showed through every so often. She welcomed the break for photographs...until the photographer explained what he wanted.

"Think casual and warm," he said. "Sprawled on the couch in each other's arms, sharing confidences after a hard day's work."

Given the heavy rain outside and the already darkening late-afternoon sky, the house did feel cozy and warm. Jake had built a fire before the reporter arrived, and the crackle of flames and rustle of settling wood made for a, well, romantic sound track.

"Just pretend I'm not here," Kara chirped, her pen poised.

As Sabrina perched on top of Jake, trying not to dig

her elbows into his chest, she muttered, "I suppose you share confidences in this position all the time."

"It's a favorite," he agreed. His breath stirred a lock of hair that kept falling onto his face.

"That must be irritating," she observed.

"I'll cope." He blew a puff of air that set her hair swaying. "So, dear, how was your day?"

Sabrina giggled at the preposterousness of it all. "Strenuous. A haircut and a manicure."

"Poor sweetheart."

She flashed her nails at him. "Pink Passion, what do you think?"

"Intriguing," he said.

"Really?" She drew back. "I think it's a little tame."

His eyes weren't on her nails. Instead, he was focused on the opening of her blouse—in their current position, he could see right down her front. "Jake!" She felt color in her cheeks.

"Not tame at all," he said, not shifting his gaze.

"Sabrina, can you move up so your face is nearer Jake's?" the photographer asked.

She squirmed her way up his body...and realized he was holding himself rigid, his jaw clenched as if he was in pain. Now, *that* was intriguing.

"Like this?" she asked the photographer. She wriggled down a little. "Or is this better?" Another wriggle. "How about this?"

Jake's large hand clamped over her jean-clad derriere. "Move one more inch," he murmured, "and I won't be held responsible for my actions."

She couldn't have moved if her life depended on it. Not with his hand cupping her, his thumb tracing the curve of her bottom. "Jake," she whispered. She'd intended a protest, but it came out a plea.

"Got it," the photographer chirped. "Now let's have you both in the kitchen, making a good old PB sandwich together."

"I'm allergic," Sabrina lied. Only to have the photographer insist on cheese.

IN THE NEXT ROUND of questions, Kara wanted details of their grand romance. Jake held Sabrina's hand on the couch the way a fiancé should, but his answers dwindled to distracted monosyllables. Beside him, Sabrina kept up a flow of chatter. She was used to these kinds of questions, he supposed.

What the hell had happened back there? How had he ended up desperate to make love to a woman he didn't trust, didn't particularly like? Now, holding her hand felt like a poor substitute for touching her all over. Dammit, he didn't want this—this chemistry between them.

"Last question, Jake," Kara said. "It's a biggie. What do you love most about Sabrina?" She sat, pen poised, eyes bright.

What kind of question was that? Who would be dumb enough to answer?

Evidently, *he* was expected to be that dumb. Sabrina's grip tightened imperceptibly on his hand. The reporter cocked her head.

"I, uh…" His throat clogged. Dammit, he *didn't* love Sabrina. Jake pulled free and spread his hands in her direction. "Look at her," he said. "What's not to love?"

Right away, he knew he'd given the answer Sabrina would hate most. He'd said he loved her looks. Just like everyone else in the world.

Sabrina's face paled to porcelain; her smile set like stone. The disappointed reporter made a note on her pad.

Jake cursed inwardly. Too late to change it now.

"What about you, Sabrina?" Kara said hopefully. "What do you love most about Jake?"

He half expected her to return the insult. Sabrina thought for a long moment. So long that he started to worry. Then she turned a smile on him. As always, it was beautiful…but her eyes glittered.

"That's easy, Kara," she said.

Uh-oh. Jake took her hand again, applied pressure.

"The thing I love most about Jake is his unswerving commitment to me," Sabrina said.

Where was she going? He was damn sure it was nowhere harmless.

"Not just to our future together, but to everything that matters to me," Sabrina said. "In particular to my work for the Injured Kids Education Trust."

He fought the urge to clamp a hand over her mouth. "Sabrina," he said tightly.

"Tell me more," the reporter invited.

"Jake understood immediately the impact the school will have on its students," Sabrina said. "From day one of my involvement, he's promised that if he's elected governor, the Injured Kids Education Trust will have his support for one hundred percent state funding." She beamed at Jake, and sighed the sigh of a besotted romantic. "What's not to love?"

"YOU WERE OUT OF LINE," Jake yelled, the moment the reporter was in her car. He grabbed the bourbon from the drinks cabinet in the living room and poured himself a generous slug.

"You were a jerk. How dare you tell her you're marrying me for my looks?" Sabrina shook with... anger. Not hurt. She wasn't about to let Jake hurt her again.

She stomped to the kitchen, Jake on her heels.

"I'm going to call her right now and tell her I don't support your school," he said.

"When you're done, hand the phone over to me and I'll tell her we're not really engaged."

He slammed his bourbon glass down on the island. "You wouldn't."

"Try me. I busted a gut through that interview, being nice while you grunted at her. And you repaid me with the worst possible insult."

He threw his hands in the air. "I said you're beautiful. Since when is that an insult? And I did not grunt."

Sabrina wasn't about to argue with such patent idiocy. She turned her back on him, and caught her reflection in the French doors. Her hair was a mess— surely it hadn't looked like that in the photos? She patted it down.

Jake grabbed her arm, tugged her to face him. "If you don't want people focusing on your looks, quit staring in the mirror every two minutes. I saw you checking your makeup in your breakfast spoon this morning."

"I didn't—" Actually, she probably did. Even now, the compulsion to turn back to the French doors and see if she'd fixed her hair properly was almost impossible to resist.

He picked up his bourbon, took a more considered swig. "You're obsessed with your appearance," he accused. The light in his eye said he was staking a claim to the moral high ground.

Over her dead body.

"My appearance is all I have," she snapped. "I'm *playing* to my strength. I don't have a great education, Jake. People don't hang out to hear my opinions."

"You seem plenty opinionated to me. You made up a whole bunch of opinions for me with that journalist." But the heat had gone out of his voice.

"People listen to me because they like the way I look," she said. "Being beautiful is what I do best, and I take it seriously."

"You're good at other things." He tossed back the rest of the bourbon.

"Name one—and don't you dare say cooking."

"You have plenty going for you, so don't fish for compliments. There was that paper you wrote for the education department, for a start." The doorbell rang; he cursed. "If it's that reporter, you can set her straight about those lies you told."

"It'll be Susan," Sabrina said. "She's been so excited about the *Southern Woman* interview, she'll have come to see how it went."

She followed Jake into the entrance hall. Sure enough, Susan came in, shaking her umbrella over the doormat.

"It's awful out there," Susan said. "But the good news is, I had a call from Kara Simons, and she said you two were wonderful interviews."

As Jake moved to shut the door, a white Toyota Corolla swung into the driveway behind Susan's Lexus.

"Who's that?" Sabrina asked.

Jake squinted into the driving rain. The car's lights went out, the driver's door opened. A man emerged, holding a newspaper over his head, scant protection against the wet. "I can't see," Jake said.

The mystery visitor didn't drop the newspaper until he reached the haven of the front porch.

Sabrina clapped a hand to her mouth; Susan squawked.

Jake's heart stopped for a moment. He ran a hand over his face, willing this to be a hallucination.

Not a hallucination.

His father.

"What the hell?" Jake should slam the door on Ted, but he couldn't drag his eyes from the face that was almost as familiar as his own.

Ted stared at Jake. He ran shaking hands through his damp hair, his breathing heavy. Then he grinned. "Son, it's great to see you."

Thrown off balance, Jake steadied himself with a hand on the doorjamb. Ted sounded different, his voice less modulated, emotion thrumming beneath the words. But he looked the same.

Too much the same. Jake didn't detect any ravages—either from shame or guilt. If anything, his father's color was healthier, though through the damp it seemed his salt-and-pepper hair was now more gray than brown. Other than that, it could have been last week that his father had left. The hurt and anger felt raw enough for it.

Jake folded his arms and put enough hostility into the space around him to check a small army. Ted's hands, which he'd raised, fell to his sides.

"You look good," Ted said.

"Dad…" Jake cleared his throat. "Why are you here?"

Sabrina tugged on his arm. "Jake, ask him in. Someone might see."

She was right. The neighbors returned home from work about now. Though it was almost dark, Jake couldn't risk anyone seeing him chatting to his father on the doorstep. He stepped aside, jerked his head in sullen invitation.

Ted focused on scuffing his shoes on the doormat, rather than on the resentment that hardened his son's face. The brisk movement, the simple courtesy steadied his nerves. He stepped over the threshold he'd begun to wonder if he might never cross.

Sabrina was there, clinging to Jake as he'd known she would be. He nodded to her. No point antagonizing her, or Jake, before he had a chance to say his piece. Behind Sabrina was… "Susan."

The glow from the overhead light caught her hair, a

shade lighter than it had been five years ago. He guessed she colored it to keep the gray at bay—she must be, what, fifty-seven by now? She was still in good shape, thicker at the waist, but with enough definition to her figure to qualify comfortably at the womanly end of the scale, rather than matronly. Her ankles were still disproportionately slender, her calves shapely where her rich, plum-colored skirt ended. Ted had always admired Susan's ankles.

She stood stiff and still, hands fisted at her sides. "How could you do this, Ted? Come back, *now?*"

He'd hurt her almost as much as he'd hurt his son and Leah, his wife. He touched her shoulder, a gesture of apology that made her flinch. Ted shook his head; Susan wasn't a priority tonight.

He followed Jake into the living room, a massive space he knew instinctively his son had designed. Ted drank it in with greedy eyes.

Jake crossed to a bourbon bottle open on the sideboard. He pulled out a glass, poured a large measure. "Want one?"

"No. Thank you." He'd been driving so long he was almost dead on his feet. Jake hadn't invited him to sit; a bourbon would knock him flat.

Jake chugged back a healthy swallow. Did he drink too much? Ted had no idea.

"What will it take to get you to leave?" Jake asked.

Sabrina gasped.

Ted kept his voice even. "Your fiancée thinks we should talk."

Sabrina made an inarticulate half gurgle, half whimper.

Jake's fingers tightened around the glass. "Don't drag Sabrina into this."

She gripped the back of the couch, behind where Susan sat. "Ted, I told you *not* to come."

Jake's head whirled around. "You've spoken to him?" he accused her.

She recoiled. "Those phone calls I thought were Tammy. Turned out it was your dad. He wanted to talk. I thought it was something you needed to do, but not now." Ted could see that her excuse wasn't remotely acceptable to his son, who set impossible standards. Maybe this mission wouldn't be so difficult, after all.

"Why didn't you tell me?" Jake took a slug of bourbon, emptying the glass. "What game are you playing now, Sabrina?"

Susan's eyes widened at the venom in Jake's tone, but Ted welcomed it.

Sabrina rubbed her arms despite the heat from the massive fireplace. "I knew you were still mad at Ted. I didn't want you to do anything that might make things worse between you."

Ted sensed the time was right. "Jake, you asked what it would take to get me to leave? Break off your engagement."

"What?" Jake looked wild-eyed, which encouraged Ted to believe he wasn't used to knocking back the bourbon so fast.

"Jake, I came to warn you that if you marry that

girl—" he spoke as if Sabrina wasn't in the room "—you'll be miserable from the first day to the last."

Sabrina paled, but didn't say anything. Susan made up for it with a shriek of outrage.

"Get out," Jake said.

Ted wasn't ready to go, but if he stood here much longer... He crossed to the fireplace, put a hand on the mantelpiece. The heat of the fire made him sneeze, but he felt better now that he was propped up. Among the photos lining the mantel he glimpsed a wedding shot in a brass frame, him and Leah.

Jake set his glass on the sideboard. "My relationship is none of your business."

"That girl is a clinging vine," he said. "You need a woman who'll be a helpmeet for you." An old-fashioned word, a biblical word, but one he'd thought a lot about in recent years. "Find someone you can trust through good times and bad."

"Like I trusted you?" Jake sneered.

"Don't let our family train wreck derail your future," Ted said. "Sabrina kept my phone call a secret from you. I'll bet it's not the first time she's gone behind your back."

A muscle twitched in Jake's cheek. He'd hit a sore spot. But his son said, "I don't need your advice."

Ted turned to Sabrina, who had sunk onto the couch. "Can you honestly say you've done anything with purely my son's interests at heart? When your own concerns haven't come first?"

Her blue eyes were wide with hurt, her fingers

pressed to her lips. "I *wanted* you to talk to Jake," she choked out. "Just not yet."

"If you love Jake, you'll leave town right now." Susan's voice rang cold and clear. "Leave, Ted. There's nothing for you here."

If hostile vibes could kill, he'd be gone from this world. But Ted had faced far larger, far more antagonistic crowds. "I've driven ten hours straight from Florida," he said. "I'm not going anywhere."

"You can't stay here." Jake picked up his empty glass, then put it down again. "Dad, I don't want to talk to you. Not before the election, not after. And..." He hesitated. "You can't talk me out of marrying Sabrina."

Ted shook his head, silently appealing to his son with all the emotion he wouldn't express aloud in front of Susan and Sabrina. "I don't intend showing my face in public. I'm not here to disrupt your campaign. Heaven knows, it's chaotic enough already."

Susan uttered an indignant protest.

"You've lost your touch," he told her.

"Don't you dare judge the way I'm handling the legacy of your deceit," she retorted.

"Just...go," Jake said.

Ted wondered if he could make it as far as the couch without his legs buckling. In a single, graceful movement Susan was on her feet. "I'll take you home with me."

"Susan, no," Jake said.

"You're right, he can't stay here," she countered. "I won't risk him checking into a motel and being recognized." She picked up her purse, the kind of huge, black bag that had served her well during Ted's campaign. He'd been amazed at the stuff she kept in there. "You get one night in my guest room," she told Ted. "Then tomorrow, you go."

SABRINA STAYED SEATED on the couch through Susan and Ted's departure.

Ted Warrington might be corrupt and a cheat, but he'd dealt her an immobilizing blow. The truth.

He'd accused her of never doing anything purely with Jake's interests at heart. For a fraction of a second she'd been fired up to defend herself, the way Jake said she should. Then she'd realized. It was true.

When she'd been in love with Jake, her preoccupation had been with how to hold on to him, to make him love her. Not with actually loving him. It was the same now. Though she'd told him their engagement would benefit him as much as her, that wasn't why she'd gone into it.

The engagement is different. There's nothing between me and Jake now, there's no reason why I should think of him.

But five years ago... She'd broken the devastating news to him that his father had taken a bribe, and her worry had all been for herself. Whether their disintegrating relationship could survive the crisis, not whether Jake's family could. And when she'd told the media...the desire to do the right thing had been part of her motivation. But, shamefully, not the main part.

"Dad can't stay in Atlanta, not even for a night," Jake said abruptly. "Someone will see him in daylight."

Still dazed, she glanced up and realized he'd grabbed his keys from the hall console.

"What are you doing?" Sabrina levered herself off the couch.

"I'm going after him. I'll run him out of town myself."

She pushed aside the unwelcome memories that Ted had dug up. "You're drunk, you can't go anywhere."

"I had two bourbons." He opened the front door and hit the button on his remote control to unlock the Alfa. In the driveway, its lights flashed.

"Two *enormous* bourbons. Probably the equivalent of six drinks in half an hour."

Jake grabbed the handrail to descend the steps slick from the rain. Sabrina followed, her shoes tip-tapping down the walk.

"Go back inside," he said. "You're getting wet."

"If you're going to run your dad out of town, I'll have to drive." Ha, there was one thing she could do purely for his benefit.

"I'm fine," Jake snapped.

"Candidate Caught in Drink-Drive Scandal," she said, announcing the next day's headline.

He snarled, but he handed her his keys and slumped into the passenger seat. "Have you driven a stick shift before?"

"Of course." She put the stick into first gear, graunched it. "Some time ago," she admitted.

They made it without mishap to the road. Jake told her to head for Susan's place. After they'd been driving a minute, Sabrina said, "I'm sorry I didn't tell you about your dad's call."

The apology had the effect of breaking a dam; his fury poured out, a river flowing not just with tonight's anger, but swelled by five years' bitterness. Because Sabrina knew she deserved it, though not for the reason he thought, she let him carry on.

"You *never* think," he roared. "You don't think about anything other than your makeup and your beauty sleep and your stupid ideals. You think everyone should be nice and live together in peace and harmony—"

"They should," she couldn't resist saying.

"Life isn't a beauty pageant," Jake ranted. "Real life is dirty and painful and uncomfortable." Fueled by the bourbon roiling in his stomach, he belched to make his point.

"Don't be crass."

"Dammit, Sabrina. Grow up!"

Jake waited for her to fight back. She said nothing. What was wrong with her tonight? The past few days he'd gotten used to her giving as good as she got, making him realize that with him, she was completely different from the way she was with her family.

"I'd end this engagement in a heartbeat and see you thrown out of your job," he said to goad her.

Silence.

"But if it comes to a toss-up over who's less welcome in my life—you or my father—Dad wins," he said bitterly. No reply. "Though it's a damn close contest," he thundered, aware he sounded as childish as he'd accused her of being.

She kept her eyes on the road, refused to even glance at him. Nausea washed over him; Jake settled back in his seat, closed his eyes. Maybe he *had* drunk too much. He'd sober up, make sure he was as coldly coherent as he needed to be, then tear another strip off her.

Through his bourbon haze, he realized something was wrong with the car. He opened his eyes. "That's all I need," he muttered.

"What's that?" Sabrina didn't look away from the road. She sat forward, gripping the steering wheel.

"The engine's lost power."

She glanced at the dash. "We're doing twenty-five, it feels about right."

Jake straightened. "We're doing twenty-five miles an hour?"

Another glance at the dash. "Uh-huh."

He looked out his side window, searching the darkness for road repairs or some catastrophe that would have lowered the speed limit. "This is a thirty-mile area."

She frowned, leaned closer to the steering wheel. "I never drive that fast on these roads."

"*These* roads?"

"Roads with a thirty-mile limit."

"What?" The alcohol decided to add a headache to his list of injuries.

"Don't distract me," she said urgently. She looked about ninety years old now, hunched over the wheel, peering into the night.

"We're supposed to be *chasing* my father," he said. "You can't run someone out of town at twenty-five miles per hour." He rubbed his throbbing temples. "Sabrina, pull over."

She swerved into the curb, braking far more sharply than she needed to at this speed. "Do you need to throw up?"

He did, but that was beside the point. "Answer me. Why are you driving like a geriatric snail?"

"This is how I always drive." She put her hand on the gear stick, ready to shift. "If this is a car chase, we'd better go."

She was getting nuttier by the minute. He put his hand over hers. Purely to stop her. "Answer the question."

She glanced down at his hand, then at the road ahead. "I'm a naturally cautious driver."

"There's cautious, and there's weird." His headache picked up, and he started ranting again. "Can't you do anything like a normal person? No, that would be too hard. Heaven forbid Sabrina Merritt should do something without attracting attention to herself."

He went on in that vein for a minute, but he wasn't really enjoying it.

"Jake," she yelled so suddenly that he shut up. Had he ever heard Sabrina yell before?

"I-can't-risk-having-another-accident," she said in a rush.

Jake's fogged brain separated the words, grappled with the meaning. "You're not saying—" maybe he was drunker than he thought "—you're afraid that if you drive at thirty miles per hour you'll crash the car, are you?"

"Not specifically," she hedged.

In his current state, it was enough to confuse him. "You risk crashing every time you get in a car, no matter how fast you're going."

She shuddered.

"Everyone does." He rubbed his forehead. "Let me get this straight. Because you got hurt in an accident ten years ago, you drive everywhere at twenty-five miles an hour?"

"For someone considered so smart, you're remarkably slow to absorb this," she said.

He couldn't remember if she'd driven him anywhere when they were dating—she couldn't have. Even when he was crazy about her he'd have noticed such odd behavior.

"If you must know, I usually drive nearer twenty miles an hour," she said. "Tonight, I'm aware you're in a hurry." Again, she tried to shift into first gear, but he tightened his grip on her hand, remembering how fast he'd driven with her to their various appointments the past few days. Usually trying to make up time lost while she finished her beauty sleep and her makeup.

"Are you terrified when I drive you?" he said roughly.

She shook her head and his chest eased. "I'm never conscious of the risk when someone else is behind the wheel."

That didn't make sense. "You weren't driving when your mom died, were you?"

She shook her head again. "It's not about Mom, this is all about me." She gave him the ghost of a smile. "Which wouldn't surprise you or your dad."

"Leave him out of it," Jake growled.

She bit her lip, though not hard enough to mess her lipstick. "I know my attitude isn't logical—the crash wasn't Mom's fault, the other driver was changing stations on his radio and didn't see us. But it took me so long to recover from the accident, whenever I get behind the wheel I just freeze up." She jiggled the gearstick. "I couldn't go through that again."

Her fingers felt chilled; Jake prized her hand loose and chafed it between his. His head started to clear. "The odds of an accident like that happening twice…"

She turned the wipers to full speed to clear the rain off the windshield. "I know, I'm an idiot."

"Didn't I tell you that you have to take yourself seriously?"

"Was that before or after you told that reporter you love me for my looks?"

He swore. "I'm sorry, all right?"

"Very gracious."

"You more than got your revenge with that stunt about your school." He released her hand. "Is there any chance we can continue this journey at a faster pace?"

"I don't think so." She pulled out from the curb and resumed crawling. "But, um, if it makes you feel better, we're not actually chasing your father."

"What do you mean?"

"I don't want you saying something—something

irrevocable while you're drunk. I have no intention of taking you to him."

"Dammit, Sabrina..."

"Sorry," she said, unrepentant.

"Where *are* we going?"

"I figured we'd drive around in circles until you fall asleep."

Instead of being outraged, Jake found himself suppressing laughter. Sabrina didn't take her eyes from the road, but she smiled.

"I'm drunker than I thought," Jake grumbled. He should be mad at her—he *was* mad at her—and yet...and yet, it wasn't that simple. Nothing about Sabrina, or this mess she'd dragged him into, was simple.

She negotiated a traffic island with the level of care Jake would have applied to defusing a bomb. "It's a shame we can't tell Ted our engagement is fake," she said, "and set his mind at rest. If he'd realized what you really meant when you said there was no way he could stop you marrying me..."

"Why should his mind get any rest?" Jake yawned, exhausted from today's emotional extremes. He would deal with all this tomorrow. He had no idea how, but he would.

CHAPTER EIGHT

"IF YOU CARE ABOUT JAKE," Susan said, "leave town now. Tonight. Please, Ted."

Despite what she'd said about taking him home, she didn't want him here. He'd only had to step over her doorstep for her to feel as if she was choking on the old betrayal.

Ignoring her, he looked into her living room from the entryway. The furniture hadn't changed since he left, but the velvet curtains were new, and so was the painting above the fireplace.

She took the opportunity to observe him. He was thinner than he used to be. He'd never been a bulky man, but now he bordered on lean. His features—the intense blue eyes and strong chin she remembered—seemed less defined. Maybe that happened when a man lost his character.

"Your arrival is a disaster for Jake's campaign. Until recently, he's been running last because people don't trust him to be more honest than you. Now, just as he starts to pick up…"

Ted didn't flinch—the man had no shame. "Maybe

he's running last because your campaign strategy is flawed."

Stiffly, she turned away from him and stowed her umbrella in the terracotta urn behind the front door.

"You used to be the best campaigner in the business, Susan. But from what I can see, you've overlooked some fundamentals."

She was sorely tempted to ask him what they were. She knew she was out of date on some of the latest text-message and Internet-based tools. Her shoes were damp, but she didn't want to remove them with Ted here. She flexed her toes and decided she could survive the discomfort. "You blew any prospect for getting involved in Jake's campaign long ago. He doesn't want you here."

"I can't leave," Ted said, slipping out of his own shoes with no qualms, "as long as Jake plans on marrying that girl."

"Sabrina is wonderful, she's perfect for Jake." She turned on her soggy heel. "I'll make sure the guest room is ready. One night, Ted, that's all."

When she returned from upstairs, she found him in Henry's den, sitting on the button-studded leather couch. He didn't look as exhausted as he had.

"Will you sit down with me, Susan?" he said. "Can we talk?"

"It's late."

"You never go to bed before eleven."

Henry used to complain about her night-owl habits. Her husband had gone to bed religiously at ten every night. At first, Susan had joined him—the prospect of

If offer card is missing write to: The Reader Service, P.O. Box 1867, Buffalo, NY 14240-1867 or visit us at www.ReaderService.com.

NO POSTAGE
NECESSARY
IF MAILED
IN THE
UNITED STATES

BUSINESS REPLY MAIL

FIRST-CLASS MAIL   PERMIT NO. 717   BUFFALO, NY

POSTAGE WILL BE PAID BY ADDRESSEE

THE READER SERVICE
PO BOX 1867
BUFFALO NY 14240-9952

Play the Lucky Hearts Game

and get...
2 FREE BOOKS and
2 FREE Mystery GIFTS...
YOURS to KEEP!

yes! I have scratched off the gold card.
Please send me my *2 FREE BOOKS* and
2 FREE Mystery GIFTS (gifts are worth about $10).
I understand that I am under no obligation to purchase
any books as explained on the back of this card.

Scratch Here!
Then look below to see what your
cards get you....*2 Free Books
& 2 Free Mystery Gifts!*

We want to make sure we offer you the best service suited to your needs. Please answer the
following question:
About how many NEW paperback fiction books have you purchased in the past 3 months?
❏ 0-2   ❏ 3-6   ❏ 7 or more

❏ **I prefer the regular-print edition**   ❏ **I prefer the larger-print edition**
336 HDL EZV7   135 HDL EZWV   339 HDL EZWK   139 HDL EZW7

FIRST NAME	LAST NAME

ADDRESS

APT.	CITY

STATE / PROV.	ZIP/POSTAL CODE

Visit us online at
www.ReaderService.com

Twenty-one gets you
2 FREE BOOKS and
2 FREE MYSTERY GIFTS!

Twenty gets you
2 FREE BOOKS!

Nineteen gets you
1 FREE BOOK!

TRY AGAIN!

▼ DETACH AND MAIL CARD TODAY! ▼

(H-SR-09/09)

® and ™ are trademarks owned and used by the trademark owner and/or its licensee.

lovemaking made an early night attractive. As they'd aged, they hadn't made love with quite the same frequency, and she'd taken to coming to bed later several times a week. Sometimes much later, though Henry, the soundest of sleepers, hadn't known that.

Since Henry's death three years ago, she hadn't shared her bed with anyone and there was no reason to retire any time other than when she wanted. She seldom went to bed before midnight these days.

"I suppose we could have a nightcap," she said.

"A brandy." His voice lifted in acknowledgment of evenings they'd shared in the past. Late-night campaign-trail drinks.

"I'll have to send Mitzy out to do her ablutions first." Ignoring Ted's smile at her delicacy of phrase, Susan went to the kitchen and shooed the desperate dog outside. When she returned to the den, to Ted, she poured two tumblers and handed one to him. She took the armchair that had been Henry's, inhaling the smell of old leather. "Why didn't you let us know you were in Florida, Ted? None of us had any idea."

"I would have told Jake if he'd replied to any of my e-mails. As it is, I've been living a blessedly anonymous life as Edward Johnson."

His mother's maiden name.

"What have you been doing all this time?"

He smiled faintly at her suspicious tone. "I breed orchids."

She adored orchids, she had a greenhouse full of them. No matter that Ted had always grown them, too, she felt outraged, as if by breeding her favorite flower he was contaminating it. "What—what kind of orchids?"

"Mostly warm-class varieties," he said. "Paphiopedilum and Vandas, in particular. The joy of being in Florida is the outdoor growing, of course."

She felt a pang of envy. His smile warmed, sympathetic rather than gloating.

"The real challenge," he said, "has been to produce my own hybrid. This year, it flowered for the first time. I hope to have it propagated for sale in the next ten years."

"Your own hybrid." No hiding her envy now. "Would I know it?" She made sure to keep up with the new hybrids entered in the American Orchid Society awards, so if he'd... Then she realized, and sucked in a breath.

"Johnsonara," she said, at the same time Ted did.

He beamed.

Under the modern naming convention, new hybrids derived from more than three orchid genera were given the last name of the person who registered them, plus the Latin ending *ara*. It made for clunky-sounding names for some very beautiful flowers.

Susan wondered that Ted hadn't used the Warrington name. *Warringtonara* might have been some small restitution for the damage he'd done, given that Johnsonara had won a national award a couple of months ago. "It's a stunning bloom," she admitted.

He nodded. "Mauve, with deep purple veins and quite a distinctive—"

"Peach speckle," she said. She'd visited the exhibition of award winners in Washington, D.C. "Beautifully uniform, those ruffled margins on the dorsal sepal and petals."

"Thank you."

Still, she struggled to accept that Ted Warrington could be the creator of one of the most beautiful flowers she'd seen. He'd always been passionate about his garden, the two of them had enjoyed an outright rivalry that had made them good friends, as well as brother- and sister-in-law and political colleagues.

"How did you do it so fast?" she demanded. "Get a new hybrid to flower within five years?" It was almost unheard of for a hobby grower... Ted must have cheated, stolen a cutting.

"All the reading I'd done over the years told me it had to be a full-time effort, in fact, several simultaneous efforts," he said. "I never had the time to try. But after I left Georgia..."

He'd had all the time in the world. No wife, no son to occupy him.

Ted spread his fingers on the arm of the couch. "You and my son are close—I saw the affection in his eyes." Now it was his turn to be envious.

"I've always loved Jake," she said. "But since you left and Leah died, yes, we've become closer." She couldn't resist adding, "This house is the nearest he has to a home."

He didn't rise to it. "Then you can convince him to talk to me. I'll find a motel, lie low until he's ready."

"It's too dangerous. If anyone discovered you were here—"

"Some things are more important than politics." A heresy from a Warrington, but Ted didn't seem to notice. "I can't stand by and see him with Sabrina. Not only are she and Jake opposites, she betrayed him."

Susan's brandy glass clattered as she set it on the coffee table in front of her. "You did the betraying, Ted. If it hadn't been for Henry's integrity, the whole family might have been dragged down."

She remembered the day Henry had confronted Ted about the bribe, after they'd been forced to read it in the newspapers first. With a start, she realized it had been in this very room, and she wondered at his gall, that he could sit here sipping brandy with such ease.

"I can't change the past." Ted stared into his brandy. "But I want to change the future. I want Jake to know I love him."

She blinked at the raw sentiment of his declaration. Henry had loved her and the boys, no doubt about that, but he wasn't someone who'd proclaim that love. Ted hadn't been, either.

"Why don't you prove you love him, and leave town?"

"Is Jake happy?" Ted asked.

"Of course."

He waved a hand. "Is my son, deep down in his heart, happy?"

Susan wanted to say that since his engagement, Jake was transformed, a new man. But truth was, Jake hadn't been happy since the scandal, and who could blame him? His mother walking out, taking up with another man as fast as she could—not that Leah had ever been the kind of woman to put her son first. His father disappearing in disgrace.

"I suspect he's not entirely happy," she said. "But he's under a lot of pressure."

"I don't believe Jake *can* be happy," Ted said, "until we fix things between us." He stretched his arms, rubbing first one biceps, then the other. He looked fitter than he used to, but his muscles were cramped, Susan guessed, from long hours at the wheel. "It's not right, Susan, for a son to despise his father. For his own peace of mind, Jake needs to forgive me, to find something in me he can respect. And love."

To her surprise, Susan felt a lump in her throat. She wouldn't say she and Henry had had the world's happiest marriage, but they'd been content, and she believed that both Max and Tyler were such wonderful boys because of the deep respect they had for their father.

"I won't leave town until I've talked to my son," Ted said. The leather creaked as he shifted, leaning toward her. "You're his campaign manager, make it happen."

In the past, he'd been a reasonable man. Now, Susan saw his desperation. A desperate man might take desperate measures, putting everything at risk. Better to help him than let him wipe out their hard-won progress.

"You can't go to a motel. You'll stay here, and you won't leave the house," she said, planning as she talked. "You won't mend any fences with Jake by trying to break up his engagement, and they're not planning a wedding until after the election. I suggest you focus on your relationship with him, aim to build a bridge."

"And maybe," he said, "with you."

"Don't think *I've* forgiven you for your disgraceful conduct," she said. "Because I haven't and I don't imagine I ever will."

"I'm not forgiven," he said seriously. "I understand."

She suspected sarcasm, but his blue eyes were honest. Ha, not likely! she reminded herself. His voice wasn't as deep as Henry's, but its resonance gave Susan an unexpected glimpse of why Leah had said, in a rare confiding moment, that Ted had first talked her into bed by reading *Catcher in the Rye* to her. Susan found herself wondering how many chapters Ted had had to read before Leah succumbed.

She stood. "I'll show you to your room." She gathered their brandy glasses and returned them to the kitchen. She let Mitzy back in and settled the dog in the utility room for the night.

Ted picked up the bag he'd brought in from the car. As they walked upstairs, Susan was conscious of his heavy tread behind her. How silly to feel, as she used to after an evening with Henry, skittish. As if the man walking upstairs behind her had...designs on her.

On the first-floor landing, she indicated the guest bedroom on the left.

"Good night, Susan," Ted said.

For a moment she thought he might kiss her cheek. Instead, Ted touched the back of her hand. That's all.

Something streaked through Susan. Heat? Cold? *Anger.*

"Good night," she said frostily, and turned away. She heard his door close behind her.

Susan prepared for bed, then slipped between the sheets. She wasn't tired after the evening's surprises, so she picked up her book from the nightstand. If only Ted hadn't come back, upsetting everyone and everything, she thought as she found the right page. If only he had never taken that bribe... If only she hadn't felt compelled to help him now. If only she felt more confident that she was doing a good job for Jake.

She blocked out the thoughts, focused on the thriller she was reading. But she struggled to immerse herself the way she usually did in a novel.

When she snapped off her lamp after midnight, she realized the overhead light was still on. With a sigh, she got up to turn it off.

Susan stood for a moment in the darkness, listening to the silence of the house—the creak of old timber, the brush of a branch against her window. She couldn't resist the temptation to open her door and check down the hall.

A ribbon of light still shone beneath Ted's door.

JAKE THUMPED ON SABRINA'S door at seven in the morning. "We're due downtown first thing for the Tomorrow's Educators conference."

Sabrina pulled her pillow over her head. She'd barely slept for worrying about Jake and Ted.

Ten minutes later, he knocked again. "Sabrina, get up, or I'm coming in."

Darned early bird and his stupid worm. Shouldn't he have a hangover? "I'm up," she mumbled just loud enough for him to hear. She eyed the door to the en suite bathroom and willed herself to get there.

At eight o'clock, she emerged from her bedroom to find Jake outside her door, arm raised, ready to pound on it again.

"Take it easy." She scanned his face. Impossible to read his mood. She wished she hadn't said those things about the accident the night before, about driving. They made her sound pathetic.

Jake pushed back the cuff of his jacket and tapped his watch. "Supporting my campaign means not making me late for public appearances."

Ah, so they were being businesslike about it. Fine with her.

"You don't have time for breakfast since you took so long getting dressed," he warned her.

She'd never been late in her life. At least, not in her recent life. Sabrina conceded Jake might have memories of her younger self stalling for time when they were dating. She'd always felt out of her depth at the political events they attended.

Now, she could handle any occasion and she had getting ready down to a fine, if slow, art. She stalked past him on her three-inch heels that eliminated the height difference between them, letting her hips swing enough in her pale gray, fitted skirt that she knew he'd have to watch.

Over her shoulder, she said, "Do you know what happens when I show up somewhere looking less than perfect?"

He followed her down the stairs. "The economy goes into freefall?"

She headed for the kitchen and the coffeepot. Jake passed her a mug.

"People—probably the same ones you hope will vote for you—tell me I'm letting the state down, that I didn't deserve to win Miss Georgia, that the newspapers must airbrush those photos of me because I don't look anywhere near as good in real life."

Jake paused as he slid the sugar across the counter. "That's horrible."

He sounded genuinely shocked; she raised her coffee mug to him. But his sympathy was short-lived. "We still need to be at the TV studio by eight forty-five."

"I'm ready to go, as soon as I finish my coffee."

"You haven't had breakfast. If you start skipping meals, next thing you know, you'll be anorexic."

"You just told me I don't have time for breakfast."

He grabbed a spoon from the cutlery drawer and stuck it in her hand. "You have to eat."

"I'm happy to drive through Krispy Kreme." She shoved the spoon back at him.

"You want a doughnut for breakfast?" He looked even more disapproving. She wondered what it would take to get his approval. The scenario was so far-fetched, she gave up. Yet even after his verbal attack on her in the car last night, she didn't feel discouraged the way she often did with her family. It probably meant she had serious personality issues, but she felt stronger for Jake's refusal to pander to her. An hour with him, and she could take on the world.

"*Two* doughnuts," she said. Which was a lie. But it was worth it to see his eyebrows draw together. "Careful, Jake, or I might think you're looking after me."

He dumped the spoon and snatched his keys off the hook next to the door to the garage. "Let's get out of here."

"Uh-uh. If I don't finish my coffee, I won't be able to string two sentences together. Unless you have a travel mug I can use?"

His gaze darted to the clock on the oven; he clamped his lips tight while she continued to sip her coffee. As they'd agreed last night, Jake was a much faster driver than she was. For him, it would only be a fifteen-minute drive to the conference hotel. His concern was needless.

TOMORROW'S EDUCATORS was the annual conference of Georgia's education department. A mix of outside and staff speakers were lined up to give talks that would inspire the department to new heights. Jake had been given the general topic of Pressing Issues for his talk. With only twenty minutes allocated, he planned a broad overview that would raise awareness. There was no time to go in depth.

He stood with Sabrina in the wings at the side of the stage as the conference emcee ran through details of fire exits, bathroom locations and so on. Sabrina had asked last week if she could come along. She hoped to talk to people about her school during the coffee break. Jake had agreed, but that was before she'd hijacked his education policy with the journalist yesterday.

He was having a hard time summoning up the anger he'd felt less than twenty-four hours ago. He was still resentful as heck that she hadn't warned him his father might show up. But Ted would be on his way out of town by now, with no harm done. What Jake couldn't forget was Sabrina hunched over the steering wheel, driving him around in circles so he couldn't hurt himself or his father.

He stole a sidelong glance at her. She wore a deep blue–violet dress that made her eyes look amazing. The halter style showcased the column of her neck, the smooth skin of her shoulders, the high curves of her breasts. Nothing in her appearance suggested a woman whose confidence fell away the moment she climbed behind a steering wheel.

Sensing his scrutiny, she turned her head. Her dress ended just above her knees, giving him the merest glimpse of smooth, tanned thigh.

"That skirt's too long," he murmured into her ear.

She groaned. "That's the third time this week you've told me that."

"You should be showing off your legs, showing those idiots they know nothing."

"And now," the emcee said, "please welcome Jake Warrington."

Polite applause rose from the audience as Jake stepped up to the lectern. "Good morning, ladies and gentlemen, it's an honor to be here today." He unfolded his notes, smoothed the pages. Bullet points told him what he had to cover: special needs, literacy support, programs for gifted kids. Important topics, discussed in every state of the U.S.A.

But he was in Georgia, and he wanted this speech to be about Georgians. To mean something more than academic theory to these people.

He held up his notes. "I have here every statistic you could ever want relating to the educational needs of children who don't fit in the regular school system." He could practically see eyes glazing over. Jake grinned... and tore his notes in half.

The sound of that rending paper galvanized the audience.

"Let's talk about real people," Jake said. "I want to introduce you to my fiancée, Sabrina Merritt." He beckoned to her.

Luckily she wasn't the kind to get stage fright. She walked onto the stage with her usual grace and beauty-queen wave. Only Jake saw the query beneath her smile. He took her hand.

"Sabrina works for the Injured Kids Education Trust, which aims to set up a school where students can study during recovery from serious injuries," Jake began. "It's a worthy cause. But more than the facts and figures, what really convinced me to support the school is my memory of Sabrina's recovery from her own spinal injury."

Sabrina started; he tightened his grip.

"Ten years ago, Sabrina was left unable to walk, after a car accident in which her mother died," he said. A murmur ran through the audience. "Before the accident

I'd barely noticed her—she was just another teenage daughter of a family friend. Then my mom dragged me to the hospital." He'd been twenty-four, working for his dad, and though he'd felt sorry for Sabrina, he'd had no interest in visiting her.

"When we walked into her room, she was strapped into a contraption that held her upright." Jake could remember her pain-filled pallor, even now. "She was supposed to spend fifteen minutes a day on the machine, building strength in her legs. She insisted on spending at least an hour every day, though the pain was terrible."

Among the sea of faces, he saw several people wince. Sabrina said, "That's enough detail, Jake."

He ignored her. "Mom suggested she take a break so she could talk to us—" typical of his mother, putting social conventions above compassion "—but Sabrina said she was determined to get to her prom the next semester."

Sabrina blushed. Couldn't Jake have fudged her words to come up with a more noble purpose? Something like, "Sabrina said she had to walk again, to show other kids there was always hope." The way he told it, she sounded like a flake. Again.

She tried to pull her hand out of his, but Jake squeezed her fingers. "She didn't make it to that prom, or the next one. But I visited her a few times after that, and each time the hope of having a regular school life was what kept her going." Jake's gaze traveled the room, making eye contact here and there. Sabrina could see the audience was riveted.

"I know there are some brave kids out there," he said,

"but they might not all have Sabrina's courage and imagination. I believe that, for those kids, the Injured Kids Education Trust school will make that hope of a regular school life real, tangible."

Jake thought she had courage and imagination?

"I don't want this state's education policy to be about target percentages," Jake said. "I want it to be about kids like the Sabrina I knew. Brave kids who need our support to get the education they deserve. I want every child in Georgia to graduate high school and to have a shot at college. And if that means we have to go the extra mile, then that's what we'll do. For our kids."

By the time he finished, there was scarcely a dry eye in the house, male or female. As they left the stage, applause broke out, enthusiastic from the beginning, but building to tumultuous.

JAKE SUGGESTED A WALK in the park across the road from the conference hotel after his presentation. He needed to call Susan, to check that his father had left town safely. He couldn't guarantee privacy in the hotel lobby, and Sabrina wouldn't let him make the call while he was driving.

"I can't believe you gave that speech," Sabrina said as they walked in the shade of plane trees so big they almost formed a tunnel over the path. The spring sunlight struggled to penetrate the canopy, dappling patches of light among the shadow.

Jake couldn't quite believe it himself. "The audience seemed to like it."

"Was that what it was about?" she asked. "Manipulating the audience's emotions?"

He drew her out of the way of an in-line skater, one of the few people in the park besides themselves. He kept hold of her hand. "I meant every word," he said. "I admire the way you fought to get past the accident."

She stopped walking, chewed her lip in that uniquely Sabrina way, delicately so as not to ruin her lipstick. The action was subconscious, he realized, not deliberate. He touched a finger to her lower lip, traced the outline.

She froze. "Jake..." Barely a whisper, fanning his finger.

He ran his finger down her chin, then lower. Instinctively, she arched her neck to welcome his touch. It was all he needed.

Jake pressed his mouth to hers.

He'd been wanting to do this forever. This was the real reason he'd tried not to think of her all these years. He hadn't wanted to want her.

Then Sabrina's arms curled around his neck, and she pressed herself closer to him. She smelled of perfume and lemon and feminine mystery. Jake inhaled, and promptly lost his mind.

He hauled her close against him, and his hands molded to her butt— Oh, yeah, perfect...

Her mouth opened beneath his, and he invaded. She tasted incredible, and she matched him kiss for kiss. He could almost have made love to her right there in the park.

"Jake." She twisted from his arms, anguish in the word.

"What's up, sweetheart?"

"I need to tell you something."

Warning prickled down his spine, but he said calmly, "Okay."

She walked ahead of him a few paces. As they emerged from the trees into sunshine, he stopped next to a wrought iron bench. He indicated for her to sit. Instead, she clasped her hands behind her back, like a prisoner about to be bound and gagged. Like a very *sexy* prisoner—the movement thrust her breasts forward. "It's about what happened...back then."

There was only one *back then*.

"What about it?" Jake sounded harsher than he intended. Instead of the familiar surge of anger that accompanied the recall of her betrayal, he felt something else. A strange reluctance to cover old ground. Not because it made him mad, but because the bribe fiasco had created a barrier between him and Sabrina.

"I thought you were going to sweep what your father did under the carpet," she said. "I should have known better."

He breathed more easily. She felt bad for not having trusted him, but he'd reached a stage where he could accept that she'd had reasons for that lack of trust. Could even take some of the blame for the misunderstanding that followed.

"You were young," he said. "You saw everything in black and white." He lifted his gaze to the sky, where a high breeze sent puffs of cloud scudding across the sun. "I should have told you what I planned to do, after you came to me about the bribe."

"You shut me out," she said.

He nodded. "We'd been arguing more and more in the weeks before that. You wanted a deeper emotional commitment and I...wasn't prepared to give it." He felt like a heel, remembering how he hadn't been able to resist her physically, even though he knew he should end the affair.

She swallowed, and nodded.

A magpie swooped in on a foil candy wrapper discarded nearby; it pecked inquisitively at its find. "I confronted Dad about the bribe. He admitted it—" even now, Jake felt sucker punched "—so I gave him three days to decide how he wanted to handle his confession and resignation. I wanted him to have a chance to start over." The same chance he was now determined to deny his father, he realized with a shock.

"I know now you would have done the right thing." She shivered despite the sun's warmth, and he rubbed her arms. She stepped away from his touch. "You accused me of seeking revenge because our personal relationship was falling apart."

Jake didn't rush his next words. He studied the cracked paving of the path, while he formulated a response that would be just right. "I said that, and at the time I believed it," he admitted. "For a long time I did. But now—"

"You were right," she said.

His head jerked up. "What?"

She hunched her shoulders, as if protecting herself. "I had to make sure the truth came out, of course, and I didn't trust you. But the way I chose to do it...that brutal exposure...it was all about my anger toward you."

Every leaf on the tree behind her seemed to spring into sharp relief; the sudden clarity of vision hurt. His head reeled, he shaded his eyes. "That press conference, the way you set the media on to Dad...you did it out of spite?"

She flinched. "Not intentionally. But in hindsight I was hurt and angry. Telling the media the way I did was a way of lashing out. I knew they would catch you and Ted by surprise—I wanted you to be as hurt as I was." She put a hand over her mouth, as if she might throw up. Jake knew exactly how she felt. "Jake, I'm sorry. My actions were unforgivable." Though her voice shook, her eyes were dry.

All along Jake had suspected Sabrina of petty revenge and now she'd admitted it. She'd heaped maximum humiliation on his family, led to the breakup of his parents' marriage because, what, Jake hadn't *loved* her?

Unable to look at her, he stalked away. Then he spun around. "You are the—"

"I know," she said quickly. "I'm not asking you to forgive me. But I realized the truth when your father accused me of selfishness. I had to tell you."

Dammit, couldn't she have kept quiet for once in her life? Couldn't she have let him continue to think better of her? Jake wished he could wind back the clock five minutes so he could stop her making this confession. So the old resentment and anger, which he now realized he'd been systematically burying almost since the start of their "engagement" wouldn't have to resurface.

Sabrina lifted a hand. Then she dropped it, turned away. "I'm so sorry."

Jake hardened his heart against her obvious contrition. *Sorry* didn't cut it.

CHAPTER NINE

SUSAN'S ELECTION CAMPAIGN was unraveling faster than one of the balls of wool Mitzy loved to play with. The catlike behaviour was another unjustified objection her sons had to her pet.

Susan had been rash committing to help Ted bridge the gap with Jake; she'd spent the morning ordering, asking and finally begging him to leave Atlanta.

Nothing had convinced him Jake was better off without him. She'd been dreading the inevitable call from Jake seeking confirmation his dad had left. The call hadn't come, which was one mercy, but a local market research firm had produced a poll that suggested Jake was trailing in the governor stakes as badly as ever. Susan couldn't understand how her team's random polling had produced such different results. Which was right?

They'd kicked off a new phone campaign, only to have the phone system at Jake's headquarters crash. Two of Jake's most loyal volunteer workers had gotten into an argument over who had raised the most money for the campaign, and the rest of the staff were taking sides. The phone system had come back up at six o'clock that evening, so Susan had stayed late to oversee the calls, then to collate the results.

It was nearly midnight when she walked into her home to find Ted at the dining table, the marble chessboard set up in front of him.

"Long day?" he said.

Susan set her purse down on the sideboard. "Bad day."

"Did you ask Jake to talk to me?"

She glanced around for Mitzy, who wasn't in her basket by the kitchen doorway. "I haven't seen him, and I have to do it face-to-face."

Ted moved the center white pawn two spaces on the chessboard. The classic opening gambit. "Do you still play?"

"Not in years," Susan said. "I was never very good." Though she knew how to respond to his opening. She and Ted had played once or twice, whiling away long delays at airports on the campaign trail.

"Join me." He hooked his foot around the leg of a chair, pushed it out for her.

"You're after an easy win?" Because Ted was an excellent chess player.

"Nothing easy about any of this," he said.

Which was so true, Susan found herself sitting. She moved her pawn.

"Safe, but unimaginative," Ted observed. His knight came into play.

Pricked by his comment, Susan moved another pawn, clearing the way for her bishop to get aggressive. Ted smiled as he assessed the board. There were more creases around his mouth these days; and his hair, though thick, had receded. But he was still a handsome man. His good looks had won votes, as she was hoping Jake's would.

He moved a piece, then glanced up and caught her staring.

Susan dropped her gaze. His knight had sneaked up on her, she realized. She put her own knight in a position that would threaten his if he tried to put her in check.

"Your strategy," Ted said, "leaves something to be desired."

Was he talking chess, or the election? The obfuscation was deliberate, judging by the quizzical look in his eyes.

She didn't want to ask him for help with the campaign—Jake would be hopping mad—but the pressures of the past couple of days had highlighted the need for fresh input.

"What would you do in my place?" A question Ted could read either way.

His smile said, Touché. A frisson ran through Susan; she bent her head over the board.

"I signed up as a supporter on Jake's Web site under another name," he said. So this *was* about the election. Her pulse raced at the idea of receiving advice from a skilled strategist like Ted. "That was two months ago. Since then, I've had a grand total of three e-mails."

"We don't want to bombard people," she began.

"Not one of those e-mails included a call to action."

Susan brought out her bishop. "I'll talk to our communications guy."

"You need to be specific with him about what you want."

"What would you think we want?" she asked.

His knight whisked one of her pawns into oblivion. She didn't mind, she could afford to lose it. But now he had his sights set on her rook. She always hated to cede a rook, though she never used them to best effect.

Her queen would be the best thing to intimidate him, she decided. But first...she nabbed one of his pawns with her bishop.

"If people won't vote for Jake because of what I did, remind supporters that the people most hurt by a man's transgressions are his children," Ted said. Her gaze flew to his. With a wry smile he sidestepped his knight around her bishop. "Ask them to e-mail Jake with their number-one concern for our children. I'd ask them to forward their e-mail to their friends, and have their friends e-mail Jake."

"Clever." She moved her queen to protect her rook.

"Good strategy," he corrected her.

His queen came out of nowhere and lunged across the board to capture Susan's. "Checkmate."

Susan gaped. He'd beaten her in fewer than ten moves. "That was rude."

"Strategy," he said again. "It's one of my strengths."

Whereas Susan was good at lining up the right interviews and managing the logistics so Jake made the most effective use of his time on the trail. Skills that were complementary to Ted's. That was why they'd made a good team.

Ted set up the chess pieces again. He had gardener's hands, very tan against the white marble pieces. Susan glanced down at her own hands. Pale, well tended, with sensibly short nails.

"You obviously wear gloves in the garden," Ted said.

Something snapped between them, powered by the synergy of shared thought.

"I—I don't like to get my hands dirty," Susan said. She hadn't intended a double entendre...but suddenly, curiosity bit down and wouldn't let go. "Why did you do it, Ted? That story you told the media about wanting to help Whitehead..."

It had sounded like the desperate excuse of a lying man.

Elbows on the table, he rested his chin on his hands. "It was no story, Susan. I really was trying to make some good come out of a bad situation."

"You took a bribe because you wanted to help the locals who would lose their homes to a new highway." It sounded just as preposterous now as it had five years ago.

"The Newland Properties subdivision at Whitehead had been turned down on the grounds the development was too intensive for its wastewater capacity," Ted said. "Newland Properties planned to appeal the ruling. It was clear they would win, and the development would go ahead, including the highway."

For Susan, this was where his story had always stopped making sense. "If Newland would have won the appeal, why did they need to bribe you?"

"It was my influence that saw the application turned down in the first place—the compensation Newland planned to pay the Whitehead people who'd lose their homes was paltry. They couldn't afford to go anywhere else." He rolled his shoulders; she wondered if they felt as stiff as hers.

"The appeal process can take a long time," he reminded her. "Under my direction, the state would have appealed their appeal and so on. It would have taken them a couple more years to get what they wanted. For those guys, time is money and the market was booming. They offered me twenty million dollars for my immediate support of the development."

"Which you accepted."

He nodded. "I didn't want the Whitehead community to come out of it with nothing. I planned to start a charitable foundation—like the Warrington Foundation—to distribute the funds for homes and education."

"Why couldn't you have made it a condition of the approval, that Newland Properties set up a fund for the residents?"

"It's been done before," Ted conceded. "But invariably the money ends up going to the wrong people, to the ones who manipulate the system. The way I planned it, I'd have had the final say over where the money went. I'd have said it was Warrington money—no one would have questioned it."

"Henry would have," Susan said.

"He didn't know the full extent of my finances."

"So, you took the money." She reminded herself they were talking about a crime here, not a social-welfare project.

"I *agreed* to take the money," he said. "Sabrina blew the whistle before the payment was made."

They fell silent. Susan remembered the chaos, the pain of what had followed.

Ted knuckled his cheeks. "I don't blame Sabrina for reporting me. But the way she did it still rankles. She claimed to love Jake, but she didn't spare his feelings one second's consideration. Didn't hesitate to destroy his family."

"She was young," Susan said uncomfortably.

"In one way, I was lucky she spoke up when she did," Ted said. "Because I hadn't yet taken the money, there wasn't enough evidence to secure a conviction. Or a jail sentence. But I paid for what I did, Susan."

The bleakness in his voice moved her. Awkwardly, she pushed the chessboard toward the center of the table and spent a few seconds getting it exactly straight.

"She broke Jake's heart, you know," he said.

Susan blinked. "Sabrina was the heartbroken one. She was mad about him. He always played it much cooler."

Ted nodded. "Jake doesn't wear his emotions on his sleeve. Buries them so deep, you wonder if he has them."

"I don't think Leah had them at all." Susan clapped a hand to her mouth. "Ted, I'm sorry. She was your wife, I shouldn't have said that."

He used his handkerchief to wipe a splash of water from the table's surface. Then he buffed the spot with a slow deliberation that for some odd reason put Susan on tenterhooks.

"Everyone knows Leah and I got married because we

had Jake on the way," he said at last. "Physical attraction brought us together, and she was the right kind of wife for a politician. But I wasn't the right man for Leah. Or the governor job. My new life focuses on the simple things, and I like that. Dirt beneath my fingers, the beauty of a flower in the first stages of bloom."

"Didn't you miss Leah at all?"

Ted grimaced. "We never had what you'd call an emotionally sustaining relationship. I think that's why Jake was so wary of his feelings for Sabrina back then. He had no idea how to handle being caught up in something beyond his experience."

Susan thought about the domino effect of Ted's crime. Jake and Sabrina had suffered. Even the cold-hearted Leah had. There was no excusing it, no matter how he sugarcoated his motives.

She was saved from comment when Mitzy scampered into the room. She must have been snoozing upstairs, even though the upper floor was strictly off-limits to her. Susan automatically reached down to caress the dog. But Ted scooped Mitzy up as she trotted past.

"Hello, young lady," he said.

Susan stared. Apart from Sabrina and Bethany, no one else called Mitzy anything other than rude names.

"I took her for a few turns around your garden today," Ted said. Misinterpreting her expression, he added, "Only the areas not visible to the neighbors."

"I didn't know you liked dogs."

"I don't," Ted said. "Especially not this one. She peed on my shoe."

Susan winced. "She gets confused."

"She knew what she was doing," he said. "She had a look in her eye."

Susan suspected he was right. Mitzy was rather selective when it came to peeing on shoes.

"She stinks, too," Ted said.

"Cavalier King Charles spaniels do not smell."

He set Mitzy down. "This one does. Maybe you'd better check her lineage."

Susan laughed. How odd, laughing with Ted. "Her lineage is impeccable." She glanced at her watch, saw it was nearly one in the morning. No wonder she was struggling to hold on to her animosity. She yawned. "I'll put Mitzy to bed, then head upstairs."

Mitzy refused to follow Susan; she lay down and began performing a hygiene ritual that no one wanted to see. Ted picked her up again, handed her over.

"Thanks." Susan pulled Mitzy in close before the dog took the opportunity to wriggle away. Unfortunately, Ted didn't quite have time to pull his hand free and it ended up sandwiched between the dog and Susan's breast.

She was burningly aware of his touch as they jostled for an awkward moment. Her face must have been beet red. Just as he freed his hand, Mitzy bit him.

"Ouch." He examined the tooth marks on his thumb.

"I'm so sorry," Susan said, appalled. Then she giggled. "I suppose she's confused again."

"Probably not," she admitted. She scratched Mitzy's ear; the dog gazed at her with soulful, innocent eyes.

"Good night, Mitzy." Ted patted the spaniel's head. He was standing very close. "Good night, Susan." He ran a finger down her cheek, then cupped it with his palm. Sensation ghosted through her—something missed, but not forgotten.

She jerked away. "What are you doing?"

"Touching your cheek," he said calmly. His gaze dropped to her mouth, then climbed again.

"Don't," she said, more loudly than she'd expected. In all the time she and Ted had campaigned together, he'd never once overstepped the boundary of their professional or family relationship. She'd never once wanted him to.

"Uh-oh," Ted said.

"What?"

"You're looking at me the way Mitzy did right before she peed on my shoes."

With a huff of indignation, hand-shaped heat still warming her cheek, and a desire to laugh firmly suppressed, Susan swept from the room.

What Ted had done five years ago wasn't funny.

SABRINA OBSERVED JAKE'S stony profile as they pulled up outside Peregrine Hospital on Sunday morning. She didn't have to see him face-on to know there were two deep frown lines between his eyes. They'd settled there and they hadn't budged since she'd told him the truth about her motives five years ago.

When they got out of the car, Sabrina pulled the Miss Georgia sash over her scarlet jersey wrap dress and set her tiara on her head.

"You're not wearing that," Jake said in disbelief.

"I wear it for all my official appearances—it's stipulated in my Miss Georgia contract." Today's visit had a dual purpose. The hospital had requested a visit from Miss Georgia to cheer up the children, and she'd asked if Jake could come along to meet some of the adult patients.

Not that he gave the slightest indication of appreciating the favor. Any accord between them had dissolved like Jell-O in the rain.

In the reception area, they met Richard Ainsley, who was a friend of the hospital's CEO, Al Greenwood. Her visit was a good chance to promote the trust's work to the hospital administration. Dr. Greenwood escorted them on their tour—first stop, the pediatric spinal unit. The kids were thrilled to see her, and when she told some of them how she'd once suffered the same kind of injury, their parents clasped her hands with brimming eyes and wordless thanks.

These patients were too young to vote, so Sabrina appreciated the way, despite his anger toward her, Jake put every effort into his conversation with the kids. Maybe because he'd visited her when she'd been in a similar condition, he was natural and relaxed; he listened with unfeigned interest to the litany of tiny breakthroughs that measured hope.

Richard Ainsley patted Sabrina's shoulder as she stood back to let Jake talk football with one kid.

"We've never had this kind of publicity before." He indicated the news crew that had come along—one advantage of having a prospective governor with them.

And an advantage of showing up on a Sunday, usually a light news night. "If you and Jake keep this up, we'll have our school in no time."

"That would be wonderful." *So long as Jake doesn't kill me first.*

Their next stop was the geriatric ward. Unlike the kids, these patients would vote in the primary. But the oldies weren't as photogenic as sick kids, so the TV crew excused themselves when Richard did.

Even without the media incentive, Jake proved as sympathetic and in touch with the needs of his audience as he had with the younger patients.

As they neared one of the last rooms in the ward, they heard a raised voice.

"That'll be Mr. Knight," the CEO, Dr. Greenwood said. "One of our more vocal patients."

Sabrina followed Jake into the room. The elderly man, rumpled in blue-and-white-striped pajamas, was propped up in bed, watching TV. *Arguing* with the TV.

"Don't believe that twaddle," he ordered the talk show's host, who was interviewing a rock star facing allegations of drug use. "Of course he *says* he's innocent. You have eyes in your head, don't you, man?"

"Mr. Knight," Dr. Greenwood said, "You have two visitors." He introduced Jake and Sabrina.

The old man's gray eyebrows beetled. "You're the one running for governor."

"That's right." Jake shook his gnarled hand.

"You're not soft on drugs, are you?"

"Not at all."

The man nodded at the TV—the sound was still blaring. "Take a gander at that hooligan, you can see he takes drugs just by looking at him." He raised his voice and shouted at the presenter. "Get up close and check out his nostrils."

Jake's eyebrows shot up; Sabrina hiccuped in an attempt not to laugh. Mr. Knight eyed her severely. "That's how you know if someone's using cocaine, young lady. Their nostrils go red from sniffing the stuff."

"Is that right?" she said.

The old man's hand thudded down onto his blanket. "I said the *nostrils*," he barked at the TV. On the screen, the host was admiring a tattoo on the singer's shoulder.

Jake turned his back on the rogue rock star. "Mr. Knight, I hope I can count on your vote in the primary."

"I'll bet you do." The man dragged his gaze away from the set. "What do you stand for again?"

"Education for all," Jake said. "And I'm tough on drugs."

"What about families?" the old man asked.

"The backbone of our society," Jake said. "I believe families need our support, but not our interference. I plan to establish a Families Commission to ensure everyone in the state has access to parenting skills courses."

"I've been in this place two months, and do you know how often my daughter's visited me?" Mr. Knight demanded.

"Uh, no."

"Once," he said, disgusted. "And that was right after I arrived. Since then, nothing."

Sabrina made a sympathetic sound.

"How often do you see your father?" Mr. Knight asked Jake.

Over the past two weeks, Sabrina had heard him tackle all kinds of difficult questions, including some about his father, with ease—deflecting the too personal, defusing the inflammatory, clarifying the confusing. But now, he froze.

It wasn't clear if the old man remembered who Jake's dad was. Not that it changed the answer.

"My father and I aren't close these days," Jake said at last.

Mr. Knight twisted his sheet between his fingers. "That's a damn shame. You oughta do something about that."

"That's what my fiancée says." Jake found a deflection at last.

"Good for you," Mr. Knight said to Sabrina. "You look like an intelligent young woman."

She smiled. "It's been a pleasure to meet you, Mr. Knight. I do hope you'll vote for Jake Warrington."

He harrumphed.

Their tour at an end, the CEO returned to his duties, leaving Jake and Sabrina to wait for the elevator.

Sabrina registered the stiffness of Jake's shoulders. "Mr. Knight was right, it *is* a damn shame you and your father never reconciled."

"Hey, why don't you invite him up here without telling me? Oh, wait, you already did." Smart aleck.

"You know I didn't invite him."

The elevator arrived and he stood aside so she could get on first.

Sabrina leaned against the back wall. "If you would just—"

"Don't start."

The doors closed and the elevator began to move.

"I know Ted let you and your mom down," Sabrina said, fast. "But you lose more by cutting him out of your life than by having him in it."

"For Pete's sake," Jake snarled as the elevator pinged their arrival and the doors slid open, "would you damn well butt out of my life?"

Sabrina stepped out of the elevator. And stopped.

Right outside was the TV crew, camera running.

"Mr. Warrington—" The reporter practically salivated; he had to wipe his mouth with the back of his hand. "What are your views on Congressman Beale's stand-down from the governor race, following a call-girl scandal?"

Sabrina clutched Jake's hand, as if they hadn't just been caught yelling at each other.

Jake tugged her close. Beale had dropped out? He reined in his galloping ambitions. Even if it was true, he had plenty more hurdles to overcome.

"You're ahead of me," he said. "I'll need to find out more details before I comment. Call me in half an hour."

"Voters see candidates' family lives as an important measure of personal integrity." Bright-eyed behind his square specs, the reporter asked, "How strong is your engagement to Sabrina Merritt?"

Which told him the crew had heard him yelling at her. Damn. "Later," he reiterated. He turned to his *fiancée.* "Come on, sweetheart, let's get you home."

Sweetheart pursed her lips, doubtless surprised at the endearment after the cold standoff of the past few days. But she allowed him to lead her past the camera.

Back in the Alfa, he waited until they hit the arterial, then punched the speed dial for Susan. Sabrina snatched the phone from him.

"Hey," he said.

"No talking while you drive." She switched off the phone and stuck it in her purse.

"Give that back, I need to find out more about Beale quitting."

"He'll still have quit by the time you get home."

She flat out refused to hand over the phone until they arrived at the house, where upon she passed it to him without a word.

Jake called Susan even before he got inside.

She picked up as he opened the front door. "I've been trying to reach you."

He glared at Sabrina as she followed him in. She glared back and headed upstairs. "My phone was switched off," he said. "I heard about Beale pulling out. It's good news."

"You obviously haven't seen the Breaking News trailer on TV." Susan didn't sound as pleased as he'd expected.

Jake strode into the living room and turned on the television.

The ribbon of text along the bottom of the screen read Call-Girl Links: Beale Out. Just what he expected.

Then: Is Warrington Next?

Jake cursed.

"You were handed the opportunity of the campaign on a plate, and you let yourself be filmed yelling at Sabrina and evading questions about your engagement. That's not like you, Jake."

She was right, he was losing his grip. Jake uttered a couple of stronger words.

"We've been inundated with calls from people mad at you for being mean to Sabrina," Susan said.

"I'm *not* mean." He was getting sick of denying that particular accusation. "Do you know that she—" Dammit, he couldn't tell Susan about Sabrina's confession.

"I don't care if she tied you up and whacked you over the head with a machete," Susan said. Jake blinked at the violence of his aunt's words. Was she stressed about something more than his faux pas? "Right now, I'd probably cheer her on," Susan continued. "Fact is, people *like* her. You need to be nice."

Judging by her careful enunciation of each syllable, Susan was furious.

"Jake?" she said, demanding a contribution.

"I'll deal with it."

"You'd better." She tapped the phone with something, probably the gold pen she was never without. "And, Jake?"

"Yes?"

"When you make things up with Sabrina, do it properly. The next three weeks are make or break. If you two have any real problems, fix them. Regardless of the election, you and Sabrina are right for each other. But I don't need to remind you no one would make a better wife for a governor."

He ignored the *regardless of the election*. Without the election, there *was* no him and Sabrina. "I'll do it properly," he said grimly.

It didn't have to be difficult. He didn't want to marry her, didn't love her, but she was attracted to him and he still wanted her more than he'd wanted any other woman.

Susan was right, now wasn't the time to be half-hearted. No matter what his personal differences with Sabrina, he had to make this real.

CHAPTER TEN

"I ACTED LIKE A JERK yesterday," Jake said the next morning. "I'm sorry I yelled at you when you were trying to make a bad situation better."

Jake was apologizing? Sabrina glanced out the kitchen window to check she hadn't been sucked into some alternative reality. Outside, the morning sun still shone and the sky was blue, not green or orange.

"And I overreacted to what you told me in the park," he said. "That business is done, I'd like us to move on."

"Move on to what?"

He popped two slices of bread into the toaster and set them to cook. "Do you remember what we were doing right before we argued in the park?"

As if she could forget! "I think you kissed me," she said vaguely.

His eyes sharpened, he wasn't fooled by her act. "That was no ordinary kiss."

Muscles tensed, deep inside her. "That's what you want to move on to? More of that?"

He opened the fridge and pulled out the butter. "I liked it a hell of a lot better than I like fighting with you." He quirked an eyebrow at her.

"Me, too," she admitted.

"So what do you say to more of that, and less of the fighting?"

She licked her lips. "I'd say it sounds like peace in the home."

"Something we should all strive for." His gaze rested on her mouth. "I'm willing to do my bit."

"So noble," she murmured.

Electricity zinged between them; Sabrina touched the fridge in an instinctive attempt to disperse the charge.

Jake advanced on her.

She flattened herself against the fridge. "I—I'm not sure I'm ready for this. Jake, you don't even like me."

He stopped. "I like you."

She slipped around him, moved to the island. "Really?" she said skeptically. "What do you like?"

He didn't hesitate. "I like that you care about other people, you worry about their happiness. I like your sense of humor. I like the way ordinary things feel fresh with you."

He stopped suddenly, as if he hadn't meant to go that far. Too late. Sabrina was already disgustingly weak at the knees.

So it was just as well Jake wrapped his arms around her.

"I like your legs," he said abruptly. "Especially your thighs. Not to mention the rest of your body." His gaze settled blatantly on her cleavage.

She interpreted his change of direction toward her appearance as his being uncomfortable with where he'd gone a moment ago, so she didn't mind. Changing the nature of their relationship would take some adjustment for both of them. She put her hands to his chest, firm and muscular under the crisp white cotton shirt. "Some people say my thighs are chunky."

"Some people are idiots." His hands slipped around to her bottom. "I'm not."

Her mouth curved. "You're so arrogant."

"Let's just say I know what I like." He pulled her closer, so her breasts brushed his chest. "Do you know what you like?"

"It seems a certain amount of arrogance...can be appealing," she admitted.

He grunted his satisfaction, and his gaze homed in on his target. Her lips.

"You're good looking, of course," she reflected, "but that doesn't matter."

"Uh-huh."

"You want to do good," she said.

He frowned.

"When you first announced you were running for governor, I thought it was an ego thing, only about ambition. But since I've been on the trail with you, I've seen how much you care about people's well-being."

She loved the color that rose along his jawline. "Most of all—" she let him off the hook "—I like that you don't worry about me, or try to protect me."

"You're not going to say I'm mean, are you?"

She shook her head.

"Because if I thought you needed protecting, I'd do it." His head jerked back at his admission. "You're quite capable of looking after yourself." He sounded as if he was telling himself, not her.

She beamed. "You think so?"

He pressed a kiss to her forehead. "Did I say I like that you're so tall?"

She pinched his butt, a reminder to answer her question.

"I may not always agree with your methods," he said, "but, yeah, I'd say you have most things in your life exactly where you want them."

She laughed. "Thanks, Jake." She kissed his chin.

His eyes met hers, and darkened to the indigo of a twilit sea. Her mouth puckered of its own volition, and it seemed he took it as an invitation.

His lips came down on hers. But it wasn't the frantic passion that had gripped them in the park. The kiss was gentler, more exploratory. Jake's tongue swept her lower lip, then sought entry to her mouth. She couldn't deny him; she opened.

He tasted of coffee and mint and morning male. Sabrina suspected the taste could become addictive.

As the kiss deepened, the kitchen was silent, except for their breathing. The metallic pop of the toaster sounded unnaturally loud. Jake drew back from the kiss, but didn't release her.

"Mmm." He dropped a kiss on her hair.

"Don't you have a campaign to run?" Sabrina asked.

"I guess. How about we have a quiet evening in later?"

Her pulse skittered. "It's Susan's fundraiser," she reminded him. Susan had invited several Atlanta bigwigs for cocktails, in the hope of squeezing more campaign funds out of them.

"I forgot." His hand caressed her backside. "Shouldn't you be getting ready?" he said with fake concern.

It was ten hours until they needed to leave. "You're right," she said with equally fake alarm.

Sabrina knew that a few kisses didn't add up to anything more than a more pleasant alternative to squabbling. But that didn't stop her humming as she went upstairs.

JAKE COULDN'T CONCENTRATE on his conversation with Sherman Farris. Which meant his attempts to persuade the man to hand over a hefty sum in campaign contributions—the whole point of this fundraising cocktail party at Susan's house—were unlikely to succeed. He hoped Farris had been paying attention to Susan's announcement earlier that thanks to some new communications strategies, public approval of Jake was at its highest level yet. He hadn't seen the figures himself, but he knew a lot more people were e-mailing him and approaching him in the street to ask about his policies.

He should tell Farris, but for that he'd need to focus on the older man, rather than on the source of his distraction, twenty feet away in a midthigh hot-pink dress that made him want to take it off her.

Ever since this morning he'd felt as if he'd had the rug pulled out from under him. That canoodle in the kitchen had started off as a simple gesture to restore the peace between him and Sabrina, to get them on to the one common ground where they never had any problems. Instead of keeping it light, he'd said stuff like *you make ordinary things feel fresh.*

She caught his glance across the room, lifted her glass to him with a smile. Jake didn't quite succeed in stifling a curse. He would have to pull the engagement back to a lighter, strictly physical level.

"Have you and your lady had a tiff?" Sherman Farris asked.

"Not exactly," Jake said.

"Women." Farris shook his head. "The only thing that can take a man's mind off them is—" he thought a moment "—death, I guess."

If Jake died, Sabrina would probably haunt *him.*

"Your fiancée is a true beauty," Farris said.

Jake growled some kind of agreement. She was talking to a man Jake didn't recognize. The jerk was leaning in close.

The older man laughed. "That must have been one helluva fight."

Jake realized his teeth were clenched, and tried to relax. Sabrina was conversing animatedly, but she didn't look as if she was flirting. If anything, she was frowning, though he knew that was unlikely. She was paranoid about avoiding frown lines.

"The best women are always worth the pain they cause." Farris spoke fondly, as if he was reminiscing. "I was one of the judges, you know."

"Judges?" Jake had no idea what he was talking about.

"For Miss Georgia." Farris swirled his wine reflectively. "Very high standard in last year's contest."

Jake's curiosity was piqued, despite the fact he didn't want to talk or think about Sabrina. "Were the judges unanimous?"

"It's not all looks, you know," Sherman said. "Personality is important, plus an ability to contribute to society. Breeding, too."

"Breeding?" The old-fashioned term distracted Jake from contemplation of his fiancée.

"Some of those girls, you can't trust them not to get drunk or sell nude pictures to the tabloids." Farris pursed his rubbery lips. "As Jonah Merritt said, there was no fear of that with his daughter."

It took a second for Jake to understand.

Jonah had talked to one of the judges of the Miss Georgia pageant? The judges' identities were kept secret until the day of the pageant. But someone as well connected as Jonah could doubtless find his way around that.

His mind racing, Jake said carefully, "Jonah's been around long enough to be a good judge of character."

"He knew a few things about some of those other girls that would make your hair stand on end." Farris looked from his wine to Sabrina, as if comparing two fine products. "I think we made the right choice." He clapped Jake on the back. "So did you."

As Jake walked away, hands stuffed into the pockets of his suit pants, he struggled to absorb what he'd just learned. Miss Whiter-than-White Whistle-blower had corruption in her own past. It was inconceivable...but true.

A couple of weeks ago, it would have been hard to resist the temptation to drop a word in the ear of a reporter. If the truth became public knowledge, Sabrina would be stripped of her crown the way Jake's father had been stripped of his office.

WHEN THE JAZZ QUARTET struck up "The Look of Love," Susan headed upstairs, leaving her guests in the hands of the very capable catering staff.

This song had been the first dance at Susan's wedding—she could remember the happiness she'd felt in Henry's arms. Not some giddy feeling of love, more a sense of security and comfort. She'd loved Henry until he died, and he'd loved her back, but it had never been the kind of crazy passion some people shared.

She stopped as she reached the landing, her hand on the newel post, wondering why she'd come up here.

She knew why. Because she was getting used to sharing her days with Ted. Most days they played chess, sometimes they worked in the garden. Every day, they talked. It felt strange downstairs without him.

She tapped on his door, and went in. Ted was sitting in the armchair by the window, reading. Though he knew everyone downstairs, he of course hadn't been invited.

He closed his book with a smile. "This song," he said.

"Yes." The tune drifted clearly through the floorboards. She took the other armchair, next to his.

He hummed along to the music in a good tenor. Susan closed her eyes, listening. Ted had been the best man at their wedding. She'd danced with him, too. She couldn't remember the song, but it was a Jerome Kern number...

"'Georgia on My Mind,'" he said.

Her eyes snapped open.

"That's what you and I danced to," he reminded her.

"Yes. I wasn't sure until you said it." She laughed. "I had no idea how prescient that song would turn out to be for you."

"I did," he said. "My parents decided I would be the one to run for governor, rather than Henry, when I was fourteen years old. After they died, Henry kept the expectation alive, and in the end I stopped fighting it."

"The rest is history," she said.

"For better or for worse."

His choice of words from the marriage vow made her shiver.

Ted stood. "Dance with me?"

She wanted to dance, Susan realized.

He took her in his arms, the movement measured, formal. As they moved to the music, Susan became aware of Ted's muscular strength, the callused firmness of his hands. "The fundraiser seems to be going well," she said. "Very well."

She felt his breath across her hair.

"Pleased to hear it," Ted said.

"And the poll results that came in today are excellent. Your input to the strategy has been invaluable." She wished she could give him the credit publicly.

"You told me." He tightened his grip, making her aware of the male hardness of his body.

Susan wriggled, heard Ted's sharp intake of breath.

"Perhaps you could...loosen your hold," she said.

"I can't," he said regretfully.

"Oh." She digested that. "Really?"

"Really."

Goodness, was that Ted's tongue against her ear? It was...electrifying. He nipped her lobe, and she jumped.

He stopped moving, and momentum carried her forward, into him.

He kissed her.

He didn't rush in, didn't storm her the way some men might. Instead, his tongue traced the inside of Susan's bottom lip, then flicked out again. Then in, then out. Just when she would have groaned, he entered, and the intense heat that washed over Susan made her sag against him. He held her, strong where she needed him to be, and deepened the kiss.

She hadn't felt this desirable, hadn't wanted anyone this much, in years. How long they stood in each other's arms, she couldn't have said. But then Ted groaned, and his longing was so unfamiliar that she startled out of his embrace.

It took her a few seconds to register where she was and that the song the band was playing wasn't one she knew. She straightened her dress with jerky movements. "I'd better— I should be—"

"Don't go." Ted's eyes were brilliant, intense.

"I need to get back to my guests."

"Then promise you'll come back here later. That we'll do this later."

Stumbling into his arms was one thing. Planning to kiss her brother-in-law was altogether different. "Ted, I can't."

His jaw set. How could she have thought he was less determined than Jake? "I want you, Susan."

Her body just about melted. "Don't."

"I want you more than I've ever wanted anyone."

"That's absurd." Because right now she felt the same and it couldn't be true.

"You're scared." His voice was so gentle, tears pricked her eyes.

"Not at all." Susan took a step backward, then another one. The back of her knees brushed against the bed. "Ted, yes, there was a moment's…wanting just now. But, no, I don't want this. Not with you. You're not—not the kind of man I would ever…"

Now there was an answer he understood. Even while her mind raced ahead to forbidden territory, imagined going to bed *not alone,* Ted released her. He paced to the window, stared out into the dark garden.

She moved toward the door.

"I know I've hurt you in the past," he said, his voice low and pained. "But I'm done with sneaking around to achieve what I think is right. I'm warning you now, Susan, I intend to make you want me back."

Susan fumbled the door handle with damp palms, managed to wrestle it open. She walked out of the room…and into Jake.

"Sorry." Jake steadied her with his hands. "I was looking for—" He glanced past her into the bedroom; he stiffened. "You told me he was gone."

"I didn't say that."

Jake looked ready to slug someone; Susan edged in Ted's direction. "You asked me if Ted got away okay, and I—well—I didn't actually answer." There'd been a dozen things going on, and Jake hadn't noticed her evasion.

"You knew I thought he'd gone," he said, quiet and furious. "You deliberately—"

"Mind how you talk to your aunt," Ted snapped.

Jake glanced around, then stepped into the bedroom. Susan followed, closing the door behind her.

"Why are you still here?" Jake demanded.

Ted's gaze went to Susan. She hoped she wasn't blushing. If Jake had the faintest idea she'd just kissed Ted… Besides, she wasn't the reason Ted was still here. Was she? "Your father's been helping me," she said.

Jake didn't take his eyes off Ted. "Helping you, how?"

"With the orchids," Ted said. Susan had told Jake about his father's new career in that same conversation where she'd managed not to mention Ted was still in her house.

She appreciated Ted's attempt to protect her from Jake's ire, but she had to give credit where it was due. Besides, when Jake calmed down, it might help him see his father in a more positive light. "Ted has also been working on your campaign strategy with me," she said. "He's had ideas I could never have dreamed of, and it's thanks to him that your numbers are up where they are."

She realized she'd physically aligned herself with Ted; Jake was glaring at both of them. "I want you out of my campaign," he snarled at his father. "I want you out of this city, and most of all, I want you out of my life."

Susan put out a hand. "Jake…"

"I mean it, Susan. I'd rather have Mitzy running my campaign than him." He wheeled around and left the room.

"Oh, dear," Susan said, her voice very small. "What do we do now?"

Ted's arm settled across her shoulders. "I'm not leaving," he said, "and last time I looked, Jake wasn't the boss of me."

Susan told herself the stab of relief that he wasn't about to leave was entirely political. Not at all personal.

CHAPTER ELEVEN

AT LONG LAST, JAKE and Sabrina had an evening off their political engagements. A chance for that "quiet night in" he'd mentioned. Sabrina had offered to cook. She loved to do it, and her cordon bleu training had been woefully underutilized lately.

The meal she planned—veal escalopes with a lemon-scented sauce, gratin potatoes, green beans and grits—wasn't complex, but its well-judged flavors would make it a "symphony of taste," as one of the chefs who'd taught her called it.

"Smells great," Jake said when he walked into the kitchen from the garage. He took one look at Sabrina in her frilly white apron and started to laugh. "You realize this is every man's fantasy—Miss Georgia in his kitchen in an apron."

"I think the fantasy has nothing under the apron," she said. Was it her imagination, or was this expensive designer kitchen inadequately ventilated?

Jake stepped closer, taking more of the available air. "I was trying to keep this G-rated, like a governor who supports family values would. But now that you mention it…"

She reached into the cutlery drawer and thrust a handful of silverware at him. "Why don't you set the table before you blow the election by letting your family values slip."

He chuckled and, with a delicious look that said *later,* disappeared into the dining room. Sabrina was grateful for the breathing space. Literally. She gulped oxygen like it was going out of fashion.

When he returned, she set him to whisking the lemon sauce for the veal. It was handy having a spare pair of hands. The sauce wasn't difficult, but it did need constant attention. The phone rang while he was whisking. Jake moved to answer it, but she waved him back to the stove. "I'll get it. It's probably Tammy," she said, one hand over the receiver.

Jake looked amused.

"Hey, Baby." It was her sister Megan. "Dad suggested dinner at his place on Sunday. Can you guys make it?"

"Sounds good. Am I cooking?"

Megan's laugh was sheepish. "You know your food is the best. Is that okay?"

"Not a problem." They chatted for a few minutes.

"How are things at the education trust?" Megan said.

"I'm glad you asked." Sabrina turned down the temperature on the oven. "I met a man at Susan's fundraiser the other night, the lawyer for a charity called The Average Kid."

"Never heard of it."

"I have," Sabrina said grimly. "They're against all forms of elitist education, like programs for gifted children. They've filed a lawsuit against the Georgia education department, arguing that the state's sepcial schools funding is irresponsible use of taxpayer funds."

"Interesting," Megan said.

"It's not *interesting*," Sabrina grumbled. "They've cited our school as a prime example of elitist funding. If their case gets a hearing it could drag on goodness knows how long. We won't get funding for our school as long as there's doubt over its legality."

"There goes another job," Megan said sympathetically.

Sabrina bristled. "We're confident we can figure out a way to beat the lawsuit."

Megan chuckled. "Good luck with that. Listen, Baby, I have to read a million files by morning, so I'd better go." A moment later, she ended the call.

"How was Tammy?" Jake asked.

Sabrina inspected his sauce, decided it was whisked enough. She turned off the element. "She asked me to tell you she's completely over you."

"Wow. Completely?"

"Utterly and absolutely." She dipped a teaspoon in the sauce and tasted it. "In fact, I don't want to hurt your feelings..."

"Go ahead."

Sabrina sprinkled salt into the sauce, then stirred it. "Tammy's wondering what she saw in you in the first place."

He burst into laughter, but when she glanced at him, his face was serious. "Wow," he said. "She's come a long way from that pitiful state you said she was in."

"I might have misread that," Sabrina admitted. "She thought you broke her heart, but then she realized the relationship had never been what she'd thought."

"Ah." Jake ran the whisk under the faucet. "I never realized Tammy was such a wise woman."

Sabrina waved her spoon at him. "Oh, yeah, she's pretty smart."

"Damn right," he said, looking vaguely dissatisfied.

Jake had lit candles, so the atmosphere when they sat down was romantic. Sabrina tried not to think about where this quiet evening would lead, but when his eyes met hers across the table, dark with promise, it was all she could do not to toss everything off the table, throw herself onto the oak surface and beg him to make love to her. She fanned her face.

He eyed her. "Are you okay?"

"Those candles. Hot." She flapped away. The quirk of his eyebrows said he knew exactly what her problem was, but he didn't challenge her.

"Did you talk to Susan today?" Sabrina asked. Jake had told her after the cocktail party that his father was still in town. Not only that, but working on his campaign. Sabrina had been shallow enough to feel relieved that Susan had deceived them, just as they were deceiving her.

"Dad's still here, and Susan won't throw him out." Jake stabbed a potato with his fork. When he put it in his mouth, his expression became less hostile. That was what Sabrina loved about cooking. Some people considered it domestic drudgery. For her, it was power.

"This meal is fantastic," he said, staring down at his plate.

"Since your dad's here anyway," she said carefully, "maybe you should rethink your refusal to talk with him."

He tensed, but she knew it was hard to get in a seriously bad mood when you were eating great food.

"If you won't do it for your own sake, do it for your campaign," she said. "There are plenty of people who think it's not right for a son to disown his father. Think about Mr. Knight, the man we met at the hospital."

Jake frowned. "You're suggesting I reconcile with Dad for political gain?"

"I think you should reconcile because it's the right thing to do. I'm just giving you another perspective."

He forked a mouthful of veal. As he chewed, he drummed his fingers on the table.

"Give him a chance," Sabrina urged quietly.

"I'll think about it."

"Wow," she said. "Thanks."

"I'm not doing it for you," he said halfheartedly.

She suppressed a smile that she knew would make her look altogether too pleased with herself. Who would have thought she and Jake would ever sit at the same table and discuss his father amicably? "You were right," she said.

"Of course I was." He smacked his lips. "Man, I make a good lemon sauce."

She rolled her eyes. "I mean, you were right to pull back from our relationship."

He stilled.

"I was too young, hopelessly naive." She shivered. "It would have been a disaster if we'd stayed together."

He set down his knife and fork. "*Disaster* might be overstating it."

"No," she said, "that's the right word. We had nothing in common."

He pushed his plate away, though he hadn't quite finished his veal. "We had some things."

"Oh, sure, great sex." She waved dismissively.

He frowned. "And fun. We had fun."

"I was so juvenile," she said. "You must have laughed at me."

"I laughed *with* you," he corrected.

"If you say so."

Jake pulled his plate back. Where had this conversation come from? And why was he finding Sabrina's admission that he'd been right all those years ago, which effectively let him off the hook, so damn annoying?

He'd been having a great evening until now. Susan had been right to suggest he mend his fences with Sabrina, this whole engagement was so much less stressful.

"Why did we break up?" she asked, and Jake's stress level suddenly spiked. "I know what I did was the end point, but like you said, you were moving away from me before that. I figured we broke up because I wasn't smart enough for you."

He glowered. "Don't be stupid. You're smart."

She snickered.

"You know what I mean," he said.

"So, we broke up because…?"

Jake ran his hands through his hair. He'd thought about it often enough that he knew the answer. "What we had wasn't...sensible. Like you just said, you were too young—no matter how old you were in years," he said, seeing her about to protest, even though he was using her argument. "You needed to grow up."

Her eyes narrowed. "So you were doing me a favor."

He shook his head. "I was doing *me* a favor."

"Huh?"

"You might remember I used to say I was crazy about you," he said.

Her laugh had a sharp edge. "How could I forget? I would say I loved you and instead of saying you loved me back, you always said, 'I'm crazy about you.'"

He'd hoped she wouldn't notice the distinction. He'd been willing to admit that she drove him crazy with her mouth, her body, her cute ways, even her emotional demands that were in such contrast with his own family's. But love...

"You were too young to know about love." Before she could correct him, he added, "Too young emotionally."

"I loved you," she insisted, and something twisted in his gut.

"Saying I was crazy about you wasn't a lie," Jake said. "That's how you made me feel—crazy. You were immature, selfish, pampered."

"I can't wait to hear what you actually liked about me," she said.

"You were also sweet, kind, funny, brimming with enthusiasm. Sexy. Just thinking about you tied me up in knots." He wiped his mouth with his napkin and dropped it on the table. "I'm not the kind of guy who wants to be tied up in knots. We were too different from each other to ever get married—leaving aside the fact you were too young—but it was getting harder to think of being without you. So I started pulling back."

Jake saw the hurt in her eyes. He swallowed. "I'm sorry. I really am."

She nodded. "Since I've now realized you made the right call," she said slowly, "I should probably thank you."

He should be thrilled to know she no longer held a grudge against him. "Don't thank me."

She held his gaze and lifted her wineglass in a toast. "Let's drink to older and wiser."

Reluctantly, he clinked his glass against hers.

"And maybe—" she raised her glass again "—to doing things better in future."

Jake reached across the table for her free hand and snared her fingers. "Some things can't get any better than they were."

Sabrina felt the leashed strength of his fingers and knew exactly what he meant. "Are you sure about that?"

A low growl escaped him. He stood and walked around the table, tugged her to her feet.

Then he kissed her.

Jake's kiss awakened every dormant instinct Sabrina possessed. She'd dated men the past five years and never once felt this desperation, this craving to be satisfied. Now, she couldn't get enough of his mouth, of the lean, hard strength of his body. Of his hands, exploring her curves with a promise of intimacy to come.

She parted her lips, drew him into her mouth, matching his hunger with an appetite that condemned every other kiss she'd had as an anorexic imitation of the real thing.

She craved him, couldn't get enough of his lips, his tongue, the play of muscle beneath her hands.

When they surfaced for air, she grabbed the back of her chair for support. She was breathing heavily. "You kiss me like that again, and we're taking a step in a whole new direction."

"The direction of my bed," he agreed. "Not so new."

Sabrina squeezed her eyes shut, obliterated the images that sprang to mind. "Are you sure that's what you want?"

"Hell, yes." He moved to take her in his arms.

She put up a hand to stop him. "Jake, I'm *not* sure."

"Sweetheart, I'm no expert, but judging by that kiss, I can say with confidence this is what you want."

"A few minutes ago I said breaking up was the right thing to do. How can going to bed together also be right?"

"That was then, this is now," he said patiently. "You also said we're older and wiser."

"All the more reason not to do anything stupid."

He looked as if he would argue, then he took her hands. "If you're telling me you want to wait a while, that's fine."

Relief gushed out of her. "That's what I want. To wait. Not too long," she admitted.

"However long you want."

SUSAN DISPATCHED HER latest instructions to the Warrington campaign's communications manager with a press of the Send key in her e-mail program. After dinner, she and Ted had spent three solid hours hashing and rehashing their options for this late stage in the campaign. As always, Ted had good ideas. But he'd also conceded several points to her.

As she closed down her laptop, Susan heard the faucet running in the kitchen, the clatter of dishes being stacked in the dishwasher.

Ted was as unlike his brother as it was possible for a man to be. He didn't do things because they were expected, and he didn't expect Susan to do something just because that was the way it was always done.

She hated this artificial situation, cocooned in her house. If she could see Ted up against other men she knew, against decent, honest men, he wouldn't seem so…alluring. As it was, he was everywhere she didn't want him to be—in her house, in her beloved garden. In her mind.

Restless, she wandered into the kitchen. Ted had his shirtsleeves rolled up, and she could see the solid strength of his wrists. She swallowed.

He turned, wiped his hands on a dish towel, then folded the towel over the oven-door handle. "Show me your greenhouse," he said.

He'd been in there before, she knew. But not with her. Susan opened the backdoor and stepped outside.

Ted followed, so close she could feel the heat of his

body. She stumbled on the path, and he put a hand to her shoulder.

When Susan opened the greenhouse door, the sweet, succulent scent billowed at her like a wave. She inhaled deeply, reveled in it. Beside her, she was aware of Ted doing the same. A sidelong glance revealed his eyes were closed.

When he opened them, they were bright with excitement. It was the same way Susan felt about this place. He took three paces, and stopped. "This *Zygopetalum* is magnificent."

It was Susan's pride and joy. "I could grow it outside in summer, but it's very hard to get the watering right," she said. "*Zygopetalum* are fussy creatures."

He nodded, and touched a finger to a petal. His exploration was so gentle that Susan didn't issue her usual "Don't touch the orchids" order. Everything about the new Ted was gentle, she realized. His voice, his thoughts, his touch. It was as if he'd peeled away layers when he'd left Atlanta, exposing the tender inner man.

"Beautiful," he said. The word shimmered between them.

He fingered the petal so reverently that Susan felt the lack of touch, the absence of intimate caress, in her own life more keenly than she'd have thought possible. She made a small noise. Ted's gray eyes found hers.

He abandoned the orchids to cup her elbows in his hands. The solid warmth of his touch was like balm to a loneliness she'd only just recognized inside her. Ted walked one hand up her spine, found the back of her neck. Susan shivered, she'd always been sensitive there. His fingers circled her nape, a delicate, welcome touch, like a spring shower on a parched garden. Like a shower that reminded you what you really needed was a deluge.

"Susan."

She stepped closer. In a last, token resistance, she put her hands up to him, but then wrapped her fingers in the crisp cotton of his shirt. She ordered herself to let go, but it didn't happen.

"Susan." How had his mouth got so close to hers, so close she could feel his breath on her lips?

She shouldn't be doing this. Susan swayed, then under the pressure on her neck moved to meet his mouth.

"One kiss," he said—was it a promise, a negotiation, a quota?—a moment before his lips touched hers.

Ted's mouth was softer than Henry's had been, though not in any way soft. His kiss was questing as his lips roamed over hers, teasing, flirting.

Then it was over, before she'd even parted for him. And instead of being relieved, she was disappointed.

What had she done, after she'd told him this couldn't happen again? This was all wrong. Susan pulled away, took two steps backward on the paving stones, her hand pressed to her lips.

"I still want you," Ted said. "Have I made you want me yet?"

Susan didn't say anything. Ted's gaze measured her.

"I see," he said. "You'd still rather we stick to chess."

Her panic left her with the same rush as it had arrived. She let out the kind of shaky laugh people do when they've had a narrow escape. "That's right," she said. "We'll stick to chess."

CHAPTER TWELVE

COOKING WAS ONE AREA, beyond clothes and makeup, where Sabrina unquestionably excelled beyond her sisters. In her father's kitchen on Sunday night, she put the finishing touches to the whole salmon she planned to poach for tonight's dinner with her dad and sisters. And her fiancé. She snickered to herself as she threw a handful of sliced mushrooms into the baking dish, then began to seal the foil around the fish.

Jake arrived from a meeting at a retirement village at the same time as her sisters turned up.

He kissed her in greeting, nothing too passionate for public viewing, but long, slow and satisfying.

Megan cleared her throat loudly; Jake released Sabrina with exaggerated reluctance. This is what life would be like if she and Jake really were together.

Megan kissed Sabrina's cheek, then lifted the foil to peek at the salmon. "Smells good, Baby."

"It hasn't started cooking yet," Sabrina said.

"Well, I know it will smell good," Megan said loyally. "It always does."

"You look great, Baby," Cynthia said. "I love lilac on you."

"Thanks." Sabrina ran her palms over her skirt. Quickly, she glanced at her reflection in the oven door. She looked fine.

Jake had seen that rapid check; he shook his head, barely perceptibly.

Maybe he was right, she needed to tone down her interest in her appearance. Now that she thought about it, her sisters' effusive compliments always covered the same ground—her food and her clothes. She wasn't a smart, high-flying lawyer, but she still had something going for her.

"I have a couple of calls to make." Cynthia ran a hand through her blond hair, a sure sign thoughts of work were consuming her. "What time are we eating, Baby?"

"Could you two stop calling me Baby?" Sabrina asked, sharply enough to command her sisters' attention.

Jonah came into the kitchen, drawn from his study by their voices. Today, like most Sundays, he wore jeans too pressed to look entirely casual and a corduroy shirt. "What's up, girls?" He jerked a nod to Jake, excluding him from the "girls" label, then inspected the salmon. "Looks good, Baby."

"Dad," Megan said in a stage whisper that made Sabrina feel like a kindergartner, "we're not allowed to call her that anymore."

Jonah laughed. "But she's my baby girl."

"It makes me sound incompetent," Sabrina said. "Which I'm not." She eyeballed him.

"Of course you're not incompetent," he blustered. He appealed to her sisters. "Is she, girls?"

"No, no." Too-rapid agreement from Megan.

"Of course not," Cynthia said with the kind of force she employed to convince a jury of a particularly weak argument.

"Why don't we take our drinks to the study," her father said. Drinks in the study were a weekly ritual.

There was an unspoken seating hierarchy in the Merritt household, and somehow even guests sensed that and took their rightful place. Jake sat in one of the wing chairs opposite her father's desk, as did Cynthia. Megan had a matching armchair without wings, and Sabrina took the love seat that Jonah had given her mom on their tenth wedding anniversary.

The conversation had a familiar pattern, too. Jonah always asked for a report on each of his daughter's lives. Cynthia and Megan invariably had important cases to talk about. These days, Sabrina had the school.

Cynthia had been offered a senior position in the district attorney's office. Jonah was very excited—even more than he wanted Cynthia to work at Merritt, Merritt & Finch, he wanted her to be a judge. The DA was an important first step along that path.

"Excellent," he said to Cynthia. "I'm proud of you."

For a fraction of a second, Megan's eyes met Sabrina's, and Sabrina saw a flash of something familiar in her sister's expression. The same insecurity she felt herself. Then it was gone, and she decided she must have imagined it. Megan was *not* insecure.

"What about you, Megan?" Jonah asked.

Megan switched on as she discussed the twenty percent growth the firm's family law practice had recorded in the past month, which reinforced Sabrina's impression that she'd misjudged that moment of seeming insecurity.

"How about you, Ba—Sabrina?" Jonah said.

Megan chipped in before Sabrina could speak. "Sabrina has a lawsuit on her hands from a bunch of wackos who don't like anyone getting special treatment."

The succinct description made a serious problem sound trivial. "The wackos are an organization called The Average Kid," Sabrina told her father. "It's a lobby group against any form of elitist funding in education. They want to prove that schools like mine are wrongful use of state funds. They're singling out the Injured Kids Education Trust's proposed school as an example."

"They might have a case," Jonah said to Megan, who nodded.

"We plan to fight them," Sabrina said. "In fact, Megan, I'm hoping you'll represent the trust pro bono."

The thought had just occurred to her. As usual, she'd blurted it out, but she couldn't think of a single reason why the trust's directors might object to the services of one of Atlanta's top lawyers for free.

"Uh, it's a possibility." Megan sipped her wine. "I guess." She sipped again.

"You don't sound enthusiastic. I know you're busy, but this is important to me."

"It's not about being busy." Megan traded glances with Cynthia. "It's a question of resources."

"The idea of pro bono is it's free," Sabrina said.

Again, her sisters exchanged a look.

"I mean, the resources within your organization," Megan said. "A case like this could consume a huge amount of time. My understanding is that all your directors are part-time, with heavyweight careers of their own."

"I'm the only executive with the trust as my main priority," Sabrina agreed. "But that's okay. I'm willing to put whatever time it takes into this. I have less than two months to go as Miss Georgia, and it's winding down already."

Megan sighed. "What I'm saying, Baby, is that any pro bono client needs to put up people with the credibility to fight the case. People who'll stick with it, even if it drags on for years."

"And that's not me," Sabrina said slowly, horrible realization dawning.

Megan's face softened. "That's not you," she agreed.

Sabrina's heart pounded a tattoo; she shot to her feet. "Dammit, Megan, it *is* me. I may not be as smart as you, I may not have your powers of rhetoric, but I'm passionate about this school and I'll fight tooth and nail for it until my fingers are bloody stumps."

Megan wrinkled her nose. "Keep your hair on, *Sabrina*. I didn't mean to offend you."

"Only because you think I'm too stupid to notice when I'm being insulted," Sabrina said. "I'm sick of you—*and you*—" she rounded on Cynthia "—bragging about your work and acting as if I'm not good for anything beyond cooking your dinner."

She sent Jake a pleading look—*help me out here*. He spread his hands to say, *You're on your own*. What had he told her? *If I thought you needed protecting, I'd do it*. He was right, she didn't need his help, even if it wasn't easy to stand firm when you'd never done it before with family. When deep down, you couldn't help wondering if the reason people protected you was because you really couldn't handle the nitty-gritty.

Her insides quivered. But she'd started this, and these days, she finished what she started.

"I've been thinking about how we can trounce The Average Kid," she continued. "I have it all figured out. And, Megan, you're darn well going to help me."

"Is that so?" Megan pursed her lips.

"I'm going to ride the biggest wave of public sympathy you ever saw," Sabrina said. "All the way to the bank."

Megan frowned as she examined Sabrina's reply from all angles. "Your injury isn't news to anyone these days. I can't see people getting worked up over that."

"My injury is old news," Sabrina agreed. "Boring." She paused. "Except for the video footage. No one has seen that."

Megan gaped; Jonah drew in a pained breath. Jake leaned forward, elbows on his knees, his gaze intent.

"You would never use the videos," Megan said.

"I don't want to." Sabrina eyeballed her sister. "But I'll pull them out if I have to."

Her father had insisted on documenting each stage of her recovery so she could see how far she'd come.

Sabrina hated the videos, hated the reminder of her accident. But the footage of her pushing herself to achieve milestones weeks or months before the doctors believed she could, her talking to the camera about how much she missed school, how desperately she wanted to walk again and go to the prom...

"There's not a heart in the land that won't melt," Jake said triumphantly. From his tone, Sabrina gathered he'd seen some of the footage. It didn't surprise her; her dad had probably showed it to Ted at some stage. What did surprise her was the pride in Jake's eyes.

"And not a person in the land who'll think The Average Kid folks are anything other than leeches feeding off the less fortunate," Jonah mused aloud. "Sabrina, it's damn clever, but threatening to use those tapes—"

"It's not a threat, it's a plan of action." She set her wineglass down on the edge of his desk. "I *will* use them. I was blessed to recover from my accident— thanks to your money, Dad, I had the best doctors, as much one-on-one tutoring as I needed. Most kids aren't that fortunate, and those are the ones I want to represent." She glanced across the room. "Don't mess with me, Megan, I want your unqualified support on this."

From the silence, it seemed no one would even consider messing with her. It was a heady feeling.

"Okay, Sabrina," Megan said, clearly confused and annoyed. "I'll represent your trust."

"Thank you." Sabrina stood, dusted her hands together. "I think," she said brightly, "dinner will be ready."

"YOU WERE INCREDIBLE," Jake said as they zipped home in the Alfa through the darkened streets. He'd been buoyant right through dinner.

"I yelled at my sisters."

"Brilliant." He stopped for a red light. "Tonight, you were the strongest, smartest woman in the room."

"I kicked butt," she admitted, smirking. "You could've helped me—things were sticky there for a while."

"You proved you're more than capable of looking after yourself. I notice no one called you Baby for the rest of the night." He leaned across and kissed her hard on the mouth. Before she could respond, the light turned green.

Jake was so proud of Sabrina, his heart just about swelled out of his chest. The incredible thing was, everything she'd achieved tonight had been classic Sabrina.

She'd made assumptions and blurted them out—he could tell she'd only thought of using Megan's services a second before she suggested the idea aloud. And she'd cashed in on the sympathy her accident had brought her. The old Sabrina tricks that used to make her seem weak had made her diamond strong.

At home, Jake came around to open Sabrina's door. She smiled up at him, still mighty pleased with herself, then set off up the walk. He watched the elegant way she moved. Straight backed. The back she'd broken, the injury she'd struggled so hard, so long, to overcome.

She'd survived the accident, survived the breakup with Jake that he knew had hurt her. Survived the humiliation of Miss U.S.A., the threat of losing her job. He had no doubt she would survive this lawsuit.

It startled him to think of Sabrina as a survivor.

"Sabrina," he called before he'd even decided to.

The urgency in his voice arrested her.

"Come back," he said. Did he mean come back to the car, or something more? Damned if he knew.

She turned to face him, cocking her head. Jake took a step toward her, then another, speeding up as he neared her.

He took her hands, looked into her eyes, opaque in the moonlight. "Sabrina, I want to say…I don't want us to be…" The sentiment caught in this throat. "Dammit, Sabrina, all that stuff that happened with my dad—I forgive you."

"What?" Her fingers trembled in his. "You can't. Not just like that." But she sounded hopeful.

Jake closed his eyes a moment, made sure he meant it. The antipathy, the resentment he'd felt for her was gone. He laughed, excited now. "I forgive you," he said again. "But it's not *just like that*. It took me far too long, and I'm sorry." He swung her hands a little. "We both did some stupid things back then. But you're an amazing woman, and I can't think of one damn reason why I should still be holding on to grudges." He was conscious of a lightening in his heart, maybe even in his soul.

"Thank you, Jake." Her words were so quiet, they almost floated away on the evening breeze.

He ran a finger down her cheek, she went up on tiptoe, pressed a kiss to his mouth. When she would have pulled away, he grabbed her by both arms.

"Don't stop," he said against her lips.

She shivered…then she kissed him again.

Every muscle, sinew, cell in Jake's body cried out for more. He wrapped his arms around her, and took her mouth with a passion that felt as if it had been pent up for five excruciatingly long years. He'd held her several times the past few weeks, but not like this. Not with nothing between them but the thin fabric of her dress and the cotton of his shirt. No resentment, no anger.

It felt…pure. She molded herself to him and it was as if she belonged here. With him.

"Let's go inside," he murmured against the satin skin of her cheek. "Please, Sabrina."

He was asking for much more than those few steps into his house. Her mumble of agreement thrilled him more than winning any election ever could. He led her unresisting up the front steps. On the porch, he kissed her again, felt her sigh of relief as their lips joined.

Drugged by her nearness, his mind blanked on the combination to the front door. Sabrina laughed and keyed it in. The door clicked and Jake pushed it open.

He swept her into his arms, and used the moonlight streaming through the glass louvers to see the way up the stairs to his bedroom.

He stumbled as he reached the bed.

"I'm too heavy," she said. "Admit it, it's my thighs."

He set her down on the bed, ran his hands up her skirt. "Your thighs are incredible, just like the rest of you."

He tugged off his tie, then settled on the bed next to her. Now that he had her here and they'd agreed this would happen, he didn't want to rush. He couldn't believe how nervous he felt. Could making love with Sabrina possibly be as good as he remembered?

Then she tugged his head down to her, boldly claiming his mouth.

Jake kissed her back. Pushing up her skirt, he closed his eyes and reacquainted himself with her legs purely by touch. Incredible.

Her fingers worked the buttons of his shirt—he twitched, needing her to go faster.

"I want you so much," he finally said in frustration.

"It's mutual." Her fingers shook. "I find it galling that I'm still more attracted to you than I have been to anyone else."

He laughed. "Poor sweetheart." He ran his tongue down her throat, and she arched against him, driving him nuts. "If it's any comfort," he panted, using conversation as a barely effective form of self-restraint, "you're still the most beautiful woman I've ever met."

She wriggled the last button free and parted his shirt. "Of course I am—I'm the most beautiful woman in Georgia."

"There is that." Then her hands found his chest, and he shuddered, burying his mouth in the hollow of her shoulder. "You're also the cutest, the sexiest and the smartest."

She slapped his arm. "You'll say anything to get me into bed." But he felt the curve of her smile against his shoulder. She walked her fingers down his torso. Each press of a fingertip struck a nerve ending, shooting sensation through his body. Jake cupped the back of her head, and his mouth met hers with a ravenous hunger that couldn't be assuaged with a kiss.

He pulled back, held her gaze, then with deliberate intent slid the zipper of her skirt down.

She groaned. "I'm also the most desperate woman in Georgia."

"Now, *that* I can help with," he said. Her hands fluttered on his chest.

"I haven't done this in so long," she said breathlessly.

"Pleased to hear it." His gut tightened at the thought of her being with anyone else.

"Five years," she panted. "But already it's worth the wait."

"Poor sweetheart," Jake murmured again. Then he realized what she'd said. Abruptly he used his arms to lever away from her. "Five years?"

She moaned, trying to pull him closer, but he didn't budge. "Jake—" she opened her eyes "—what are you waiting for?"

"Five years?"

Sabrina eyed him carefully. "Uh, no, it's less than that," she said, unsure why she should lie, but knowing it was essential.

"I don't believe you." He sat up.

She scrambled to do the same, holding her skirt to her middle. "Really, Jake, so I got the dates wrong…"

"Who else have you slept with?" he demanded.

She did her best to look outraged. "That's none of your business."

"Obviously it was none of your recent boyfriends— I'd hope they'd be more memorable than that."

"I can't think why you would want my boyfriends to be memorable lovers," she said logically.

He ground his teeth. "Sabrina...tell me. Have you slept with anyone since me?"

"Why? To give your ego a thrill?" Too late, she realized she'd admitted the truth.

Jake groaned, and it was nothing like the sound he'd been making a few minutes ago.

"What the heck is your problem?" Sabrina wrestled with her zipper. She might not have had sex in years, but instinct told her there would be no clothes coming off tonight.

"What have you been doing all this time?" he demanded. "*Waiting* for me?"

Arrogant jerk. "Maybe sex with you was so bad, I never wanted to try it again."

"That's not the impression I had just now." He raked a hand through his hair. "I want to know why you haven't slept with anyone else."

She pushed herself away from him, to the far side of the enormous bed. "For the perfectly good reason that I don't do casual sex, and I wouldn't describe any of the relationships I've had since you as serious."

"What you and I have now...you think we're serious?" He shivered, as if someone had just thrown a bucket of cold water over him.

"I— Yes." Suddenly, she wasn't sure. "Don't you?"

"I think it's only about five minutes since the prospect of any kind of relationship became a reality. To say we're serious seems…premature." Jake levered himself off the bed before he lost all reason and kissed her again. He'd been disturbed by the thought of her sleeping with anyone else, and now he was alarmed she hadn't.

What did it mean, that she hadn't been with another man? And that she was willing to make love with him now? What kind of commitment would he be making if he took her to bed?

He'd rejected the idea of long-term ties to Sabrina five years ago—a logical, justifiable decision. And while they both might have changed since then, it would be crazy to rush into something now, to imply some commitment, by making love.

Jake couldn't believe how nearly he'd lost control. Which was exactly the problem he'd had with her the first time around. And look how that had turned out.

"Sabrina," he said, "I'm attracted to you, you know that. I—I care about you, too." He paused, to see how that felt. Yep, he was okay with caring about her.

She slid off the bed and stood. "Define *care*."

Did he have to? Jake struggled to think straight. "I…like being with you. I want you to achieve your goals, and I'm willing to help you."

Sabrina's laughter had an hysterical edge to it.

"Glad me spilling my heart is so funny," he said, irritated.

With difficulty, Sabrina reined in her wholly inappropriate response. Who did Jake think he was kidding, bringing his *heart* into this? The qualities he'd listed added up to only one thing. Respect.

The whole point of this ill-conceived sham of an engagement had been to earn her family's respect. She'd never dreamed she'd win Jake's respect. And that his *respect* wouldn't be enough.

The irony was, she'd never been short of love in her life, only respect. Now that she had Jake's respect...all she wanted was...*his love.*

Sabrina was achingly aware of the lack of his touch. Achingly aware that her response to him was so much more than physical. That his forgiveness had unchained feelings she'd been successfully starving in captivity.

I love him.

Last time she'd loved him, she'd seen Jake as perfect, ignored his faults so she could make him into a hero. Now...now she loved the flawed, imperfect Jake who made her laugh, who believed in her, who cheered her on in a way no one else had. She wanted him to feel the same. She'd like to hold on to that hard-won respect, but she wanted his unconditional, no-holds-barred love, too.

"You said you forgive me," she said. "And—and I forgive you."

He recoiled. "What for?"

She wrestled with her zipper again. "For letting me think there was some hope for our relationship, long after you knew there wasn't."

He let out a breath. "Okay, so we forgive each other. But that doesn't mean we're right for something serious. I'm not willing to be part of another screwup." He jammed his hands in his pockets. "Let's quit while we're ahead."

CHAPTER THIRTEEN

TED FOUND MITZY—ALONG with one of his shoes, suspiciously wet—in the kitchen, but there was no sign of Susan. Then he heard humming, the sound wafting from the sunroom. "Georgia on My Mind."

Perfect.

He paused in the sunroom doorway. Susan was deadheading chrysanthemums, humming as she snipped. He walked up behind her.

"Good morning." The formal greeting fit his mood.

"Good morning," she said warily.

He kissed her cheek, because he couldn't get a good angle. She stiffened, then rubbed at the spot his lips had touched. Her reaction disconcerted him, and he didn't sound as forceful as he'd planned when he said, "I have something to say to you."

"Me first," she said. "Ted...I've given this a lot of thought—more than I should have, really—and I've decided you need to leave."

"What?" His chest constricted. "I haven't talked to Jake yet." He threw out the first excuse he thought of.

"I spoke to Jonah this morning. Once he got over the

shock of hearing that you're back, he said he'd be pleased to have you stay." She busied herself with a faded bloom. A quick snip, and the chrysanthemum came off in her hand.

"That one wasn't dead," Ted said. "You shouldn't cut it off just because it's not perfect."

She stared down at the flower in her palm. Then she dropped it onto the heap of dead blossoms in the basket on the floor and looked up at Ted. "I can't have you here."

"Susan, give us a chance. Give yourself a chance to get past what happened."

She drew in a sharp breath. "You've known me nearly forty years. And I know more about you than I—"

"Stop." He held up a hand. "Don't say anything that will hurt us."

She fell silent. Ted figured that had to count for something. "I know I hurt you when I took that bribe. Not just you, a lot of people. But I'm not the man I was then, and I—I feel something for you. Something important."

"Ted..." She wrung her hands, clumsy in her green gardening gloves. "We kissed. Twice." Agitated, she snipped two more mums to a premature death. "That's all."

"What I feel isn't about kissing you," he said. "Though I haven't been able to stop thinking about doing it again. And a whole lot more."

She blushed a fiery red, and he saw in her eyes that she'd thought the same. His pulse surged.

"I've come to cherish your company, whether it's pottering in the kitchen, or playing chess or mucking around in your garden," he said. "I love that you're strong and smart, and you have a big heart for your sons and mine. I want you to have a big heart for me."

"You're my brother-in-law." She gripped her pruning shears tighter. "We'll always be connected in that way, but—"

"I want to stay up late at nights with you," he persisted. "I want to argue with you about Jake's campaign, I want to walk your dreadful dog. I want to prune your garden, nurture your orchids."

Susan swallowed and blinked away tears. The things he apparently cherished the thought of sharing with her were the minutiae of daily life, things she'd never expected to share with anyone again.

Things she was quite capable of doing on her own, that she'd always done on her own even when Henry was alive. Things that were inherently dull. Yet with Ted, they might feel…significant.

He hadn't said he loved her. She wouldn't have believed him, it was much too soon. But it was clear that was where he was headed. Could she depend on him, lean on him? She'd never leaned on Henry in the years of marriage. She'd never wanted that kind of dependence before. But now, it tempted her.

Except Ted wasn't the right man. A part of her could believe he would be a loving, faithful and, yes, sexy companion. Another part of her was too aware he'd deceived her before and she wasn't sure she would know if he did it again.

She took a step backward, holding the shears out

front. "Maybe I should be over what happened, but I can't forget that you lied. I don't think I ever will."

"Dearest, please."

Susan dropped the pruners into her basket and pulled off first one glove, then the other. "I don't have the kind of courage it would take to trust you."

He'd gone pale, and Susan had the sudden urge to throw herself into his arms, to kiss away the lines at the sides of his mouth.

He reached out a hand as if to steady himself, but the only thing near him was a miniature New Zealand Christmas tree. He shoved his hand in his pocket. "Is that your final word?"

"Yes." Susan ignored the ache in her throat, in her chest, and said, "So you'll leave?"

Ted nodded. "I'll leave."

SABRINA ACCOMPANIED JAKE on a visit to an organic farm an hour from Atlanta. Susan, who came, too, had insisted Jake needed to be more in touch with rural communities.

They walked fields of corn and beans as Jake listened to the farmer's views about the certification process for organic produce. As always, Jake's questions were pertinent, intelligent, and spoke of genuine interest.

"That man was born to be governor," Susan murmured. Sabrina had thought the other woman was barely listening. She'd seemed so distracted that morning.

"He's wonderful," Sabrina agreed. "But do you think being governor will make him happy?"

Susan's lips compressed. Then she patted Sabrina's arm. "I hope it'll set him on the right road."

Sabrina saw tension in her mouth. "Susan, are you okay?"

"I'm fine," Susan said a little grimly. They watched as Jake laughed at a joke the farmer made, then quipped back. "He seems happier now that the polls are healthier. I haven't seen him this relaxed in a long time." The thought seemed to cheer her—another pat on the arm for Sabrina. "I'm so pleased you two are over your little spat. When I told Jake to romance you, it wasn't just for political reasons—even if he did almost have a lynch mob after him for yelling at you at the hospital—or because you'll make a perfect governor's wife. You two are perf—"

"You *told* Jake to romance me?" Sabrina's insides had seized up halfway through Susan's monologue.

"You know men, they get so preoccupied with their work, they don't notice they're neglecting their loved ones." Susan bit her lip. Then she saw a media crew arriving and waved out. "Excuse me, dear, I need to make sure that photographer gets the shot he wants." She hurried away.

Sabrina's heels sank into the soft, pesticide-free earth as she swayed on her feet. No wonder Jake had backed out of going to bed with her. For him, the intimacy would have been a pleasant reward for making nice to her. As soon as he'd realized she was taking it more seriously, he'd retreated. She supposed she should be grateful.

"Sabrina, over here," Susan called. "This gentleman would like a photo of you among the tulips."

Her heart heavy, Sabrina obeyed. How much of what Jake had said about *liking* her, forgiving her, was true, and how much of it was just to secure her cooperation? It didn't matter, she realized. Either way, she'd let him tell her she was smart and clever and forgiven, and all the while he was manipulating her.

Sabrina's throat hurt. She massaged her neck while the political reporter from the *Journal-Constitution* posed some questions. She managed to slip in a few references to the school for injured kids, but even to her own ears she sounded wooden.

The reporter pushed his glasses up his nose. "The cost per child for a special education like the one you're talking about is high. Some would say prohibitive. Why should it be a priority for our education department?"

It sounded like something straight out of The Average Kid's manifesto. She wished Megan was here to squelch those upstarts. Sabrina felt awfully alone.

She drew a deep breath, then threw everything she had into her answer, countering the question with a vehemence that surprised—and pleased—the reporter.

"If we want our kids to grow up with the sense of opportunity that made our country great, we need to sow the seeds now, for all children. Jake's father has a wonderful saying—'If you want orchids, don't plant camellias. Plant orchids, and wait.' Or maybe here," she joked, "I should say, if you want tulips."

She realized no one appeared to get the joke.

Jake looked aghast; Susan horrified.

"When did you last talk to Ted Warrington?" the reporter asked smoothly.

Oh, heck. Sabrina darted a glance at Susan. "I—uh…"

A couple of nearby reporters overheard and made a beeline for her.

"Have you spoken to the former governor in recent weeks?" the first man persisted.

His expectant silence put more pressure on Sabrina than any barrage of questions. Somehow, she kept her mouth shut. Then Jake stepped forward, looking at the reporter, not at her.

"My father made an unexpected visit to Atlanta recently," he said. "He'd heard the news of my engagement and decided it was time we talked."

Pandemonium erupted. Cameras flashed, microphones were shoved in his face with far more urgency than the tulips had commanded.

"Is your father involved in your campaign for governor?"

"Where is Ted Warrington now?"

"How well do you and your dad get along?"

Jake held up a hand, making it clear he wouldn't speak until he could do so uninterrupted. Eventually, the ruckus subsided.

"My meeting with my father was uninvited," he said. "And unwanted, on my side. I suffered the same betrayal everyone did, and I'm not over it."

At last, he looked at Sabrina. She read the message in his hard eyes loud and clear. *You betrayed me, too.*

Ditto, she thought, and glared with a ferocity that made him blink.

As the media dispersed, Susan alternated between railing against Ted's thoughtlessness in showing up in the first place, and predicting the immediate and permanent demise of Jake's electoral hopes. Jake took Sabrina by the hand—definitely not a sign of affection—and hauled her to the organic carrot patch behind the farmhouse.

"You idiot!" he yelled the second he was sure they were out of earshot of the departing media. So much for his insistence that she shouldn't let people insult her intelligence. "What the hell were you thinking? No, don't tell me, you *didn't* think."

"I'm sorry." Because although she had just as much right to be mad, she'd never intended to embarrass him. "I was answering a question, I was distracted—" *your fault* "—and it slipped out."

"Because you can't focus on one thing for more than five minutes," he said, disgusted.

"At least I'm not a two-faced, manipulative, double-dealing sleaze," she snapped.

He stared blankly at her. "What are you talking about?"

"Susan was telling me about the excellent advice she gave you. She's thrilled with your performance."

"What advice? What performance?" He sounded bewildered, suspicious…but she was beyond falling for it.

"To *romance* me," Sabrina hissed. "So you wouldn't lose any votes and because I'll make such a wonderful governor's wife. Susan tells you to be nice, and the next minute you're paying me compliments, forgiving me…seducing me." Her voice broke. She had to wait a moment before she could continue. "You manipulated me, just like you did five years ago. And I fell for it. That's what I hate, that I'm as stupid as you obviously think I am."

Her shoulders sagged. "But I promise you, Jake, I'm not stupid enough to stay in love with you this time around."

He stared at her.

She'd admitted to Jake that she loved him. Wasn't that just the crowning glory?

He paled. "You did it deliberately."

"Excuse me?" Her attempt to sound supercilious came out a mortified squeak.

He took a step backward, hands up as if to ward off evil. "You were mad at me, so you deliberately told the press my father is back in town."

What was he talking about? "I told you, it was an accident."

Jake barely registered Sabrina's denial. "Five years ago you denounced my father because you were mad at me for not loving you enough," he said. "Today you did it again, to me and to him, for the same damn reason."

"No." Her hand fluttered at her throat. "It wasn't like that."

A hot rage overwhelmed him. She talked about him being manipulative, but the moment she didn't get what she wanted, she'd hung him out to dry.

He wanted to shake her, he wanted to curse her…he wanted to shatter her with the sordid truth about her father's role in her win at the Miss Georgia pageant. It was the perfect, lethal weapon, the ultimate lesson in how the wrong words at the wrong time could destroy someone.

Sabrina's reliance on that pageant win came back to him. *Being beautiful is what I do best.* It was utter junk—she had a host of talents, including revenge and betrayal high on the list—but she believed it. Her self-image was consumed by her looks. How could he take that away from her?

She was saying something; Jake tried to focus.

"Don't think you can pin this on me," Sabrina said. "I made a genuine mistake this morning, and I'm sorry. But you—for *weeks*—" her voice shook "—you faked liking me to get ahead."

"This whole damn engagement is fake," he roared, furious with himself for being too weak to fire his salvo about Jonah. "Everything between you and me is fake."

Except he *did* like her. Or rather, he *had* liked her.

Never again.

CHAPTER FOURTEEN

"THIS ISN'T WORKING," Sabrina told her sisters, in the spirit of her new assertiveness with them.

When she'd called to tell Megan and Cynthia she'd left Jake, they'd been gratifyingly prompt in their response to the crisis, showing up at their dad's place with her favorite Thai takeout and a couple of bottles of sauvignon blanc. Jonah was scheduled to attend a client dinner later, so they had the dining room to themselves. Unfortunately, the traditional takeout-and-booze remedy wasn't powerful enough to fix a broken heart.

"Maybe this will cheer you up." Megan twirled some Pad Thai around her fork. "The Average Kid's lawyer called to say they don't plan to cite your school in their lawsuit. They're going after the gifted kids—apparently no one feels sorry for them."

Sabrina gaped. "That's fantastic. Not about the gifted kids, but...you think my videos changed their mind?" Megan had couriered copies of the tapes to the opposing lawyer.

"No doubt about it," Megan said. "It was a brilliant

idea, Sabrina. So good, I can't believe I didn't think of it myself."

Sabrina laughed as she put an arm around her sister and squeezed. "Thanks, hon."

After her sisters left, she rang Richard Ainsley with the good news.

"An immense relief," he said. "Though I wasn't that worried. You've done a wonderful job for the trust, Sabrina. I believe we'll get our school no matter who wins the election, no matter who tries to stop us."

She choked up. "Thanks, Richard," she managed to say.

After she'd hung up the phone, Sabrina cleared away the takeout, putting the leftover green curry chicken in the fridge. Maybe its restorative powers would improve with age. Or maybe she just had to get over this all by herself.

First up, she needed to confront her father, who didn't know the engagement was off. She'd told him she and Jake had quarreled. For the past week, she'd accompanied Jake during the day to political engagements at which they both exerted themselves to charm the public, while ignoring each other. At nights, she came back here, to the sanctuary of her old room. Not for coddling, or protection. What Jake would doubtless call "running home to Daddy" had given her space to clear her head.

She found her dad in his study and launched straight into what she had to say, before Jonah could deflect her with his affectionate comments or his concern for her.

"Dad, you need to accept now that I'm never, ever going to work at Merritt, Merritt & Finch as a paralegal," she said. "Even if the school doesn't work out."

He set his pen down on his legal pad. "But, sweetheart—"

"Never," she said firmly. "I have a job that I love. One way or another I want to keep working with injured kids."

"The firm could do pro bono work for charities—"

"No legal work." If she said it often enough, it might sink in. "Dad, I've decided my future. I'm challenging you to accept my decision." She looked him square in the eye.

Jonah blustered the protests she expected. But it seemed he recognized for the first time that she meant it and he finished with, "All right, Ba—Sabrina, if that's what you want."

"Thanks, Dad." She hugged him.

"At least you're marrying a man who can take care of you," Jonah muttered. "You can give him gray hairs instead of me." His hair had been more gray than brown for the past couple of years. Sabrina walked around the desk and kissed the top of his head. She looped her arms around his neck.

"Dad, if for some reason Jake and I don't work out—" probably a good idea to prepare him for the breakup "—I plan to get my own apartment. I need to live my own life."

He grumbled, but the protest never really lifted off the ground.

THERE WAS PLENTY TO be thankful for now that Sabrina was gone, Jake told himself two days before the primary. He didn't have the stress every morning of wondering if he'd have to turf her out of bed. Or see her wandering around his kitchen in one of her short satin nightdresses.

Instead, he picked her up from her father's place every morning and they drove in silence to the day's engagements, where she smiled adoringly and kissed him on the cheek whenever the situation called for a show of affection. They probably had a better relationship than most married couples.

He picked up the morning's newspaper off the coffee table and opened it to the political columns. The rustling of the pages seemed unnaturally loud. Okay, so the house felt a little empty without Sabrina. That was a small price to pay for some peace of mind.

Five minutes later, he folded the newspaper with a snap that bordered on petulance, and picked up the phone.

It was half an hour until the doorbell rang. Jake had been pacing his living room while he waited. Now, he slowed right down, still not a hundred percent sure he wanted to open the door. But he did.

"Son." Ted caught Jake's hand in a firm grip. He had refused to give media interviews after his return was made public, but he was no longer in hiding. He'd been surprised to get Jake's call inviting him over for a beer, but he'd accepted without hesitation.

Jake led him to the kitchen. He pulled a couple of Buds from the fridge and opened them.

"How are things at Jonah's house?" He handed a beer to his father. He meant, *How's Sabrina?*

"Dull compared with Susan's place."

The answer didn't make a lot of sense, but Jake couldn't be bothered figuring it out.

"Can I take a look around?" Ted said.

Jake gave him the tour, answering his dad's questions about the design of the house as they went. It was a safe way to establish communication without having to touch on any difficult topics. But when they finished in the sitting room, it was time to get down to business. Ted settled on the leather couch; Jake sat opposite.

"Mind if I speak first?" Ted asked.

"Go ahead."

"I apologized to you a long time ago for letting you and your mother down over the bribe," Ted said. "I want to say I'm still sorrier about that than you'll ever know—there's not a day I don't regret it."

Jake grunted.

"But there's something else that makes me sorrier still."

"What's that?"

Ted laced his fingers between his knees. "If there's one thing I've learned from being cut off from my family, it's that nothing is more important than the people you love. Your mother and I went our separate ways, and you were the one who lost out. That's what I'm sorriest about, that you didn't grow up in the loving family you deserved."

Jake was horrified to feel tears prick his eyes.

"I love you, Jake."

"Dad…" Jake wiped a hand across his face. "You don't have to say that."

"It's the truth." Ted chuckled. "Felt good. I might have to tell the truth more often."

"Maybe you could find someone else to say it to." Jake was only half joking.

"I thought I had." Ted grimaced. "But that's my problem, not yours." They drank their beer in silence.

"I don't expect to wipe out the past with one beer," Ted said. "But I hope we can move forward."

Jake thought about how empty the house had felt this morning. He didn't want that kind of loneliness anymore.

"You made a mistake, Dad," he said. "But it might be time I stopped blaming you for everything that's gone wrong since."

Ted rubbed his chin. "You sure about that?"

"Certain."

Ted pushed himself off the couch and came to hug Jake where he sat.

"Dad, I thought we just agreed…" Awkwardly, Jake hugged him back.

His dad's eyes were bright as he settled back on the couch. "I'll spare you any more sentimental moments. Just let me point out, you need more than an election win to make you happy."

Jake didn't want to go there.

"Son, is there anything you want to tell me about Sabrina?"

"Uh…"

"Since I've been at Jonah's, I've sensed there's more to your engagement than meets the eye." Ted added dryly, "Or should I say, *less* to it."

Jake remembered having this same hollow pit in his

stomach when he was fourteen years old and he'd taken out the air rifle, the one he wasn't supposed to fire without supervision, to impress his buddies. He'd accidentally shot a rare bird, a Red Crossbill, and to make matters worse, his nature-loving father had caught him sneaking the rifle back into its box.

Now, as then, the compulsion to confess was overwhelming.

"The engagement's not real." He told his father about Sabrina's job being under threat, about his polling woes and the rumors that had been circulating about him and various women. How the engagement had been a solution to both their problems.

"Some people would say lying about an engagement isn't much better than what you did," Jake admitted. "But it's not illegal to pretend to be engaged." He knew the argument was flimsy.

"I'm not in a position to condemn you, son," Ted said. "I'm not even in a position to be disappointed in you. You wouldn't be in this situation if it wasn't for what I did. Besides, you don't seem too happy now that she's up and left."

"I screwed up," Jake said. "I don't have a clue how to fix it. I'm not even sure if I want to."

"You want to go another five years without talking to her?" his dad asked.

Jake sighed. "No."

"That's a clue, I guess."

"Dad, I know you don't like Sabrina…"

"She confuses me, to be honest," Ted said. "Sometimes she's the sweetest thing. Other times…I can't get a handle on her. But maybe I was wrong about her not caring enough for you."

"She cares," Jake said.

"She reminds me of an orchid."

Jake frowned. "You mean, because she's beautiful?"

"That, of course," Ted agreed. "But it's more… People think orchids are very delicate. High maintenance. It's true they're slow growing—you plant an orchid, and if it survives it'll be five years, maybe even seven, before it's mature.

"Orchids will drive anyone with less than the patience of a dead saint nuts," Ted continued. "But if they hang in there long enough to flower, they'll thrive pretty much anywhere. They're survivors." He sat back. "I hope you find what you want with Sabrina."

Jake raised his bottle in a toast to the sentiment.

"I'm sorry my being here has hurt your campaign," Ted said after a while. Since the news had broken, the polls had been all over the place, but the general trend was downward.

Jake tipped his head back, closed his eyes. "It was always a long shot. But I did want to win."

Right now, it was hard to care. He didn't want to be governor without Sabrina…he didn't want to do anything without her, ever.

Because he loved her.

Jake jerked upright, and cursed.

"Problem?" Ted asked.

"I love Sabrina."

"Problem," his father agreed.

"I have to get her back. Right now."

"Don't mind me," Ted said.

He would go to Jonah's house and tell Sabrina he loved her. And hope like hell she still loved him back. Could she?

Of course she could, she was the most forgiving person he knew.

Maybe he should show her he was worthy of that forgiveness first. Jake drained his beer. "I need to call Susan," he told his dad.

SUSAN'S EXTREME RESERVATIONS about the wisdom of Jake's hastily called press conference evaporated in the face of its obvious success.

The conference, attended by reporters from TV, radio and newspapers, took place in the campaign office. Jake told the media he'd reconciled with his father, and that he hoped to rebuild their relationship in the years to come.

"Sabrina already told you my dad's homily about orchids and camellias, about planting what you want to reap," he said. "I'm planting peace in my home. I figure if I can grow peace there, I'll be in a much stronger position to make it work in our state."

He spoke from the heart, without regard for what anyone might think. All that mattered was that Sabrina would see he was doing the right thing. But he got such an enthusiastic response from the normally cynical media, Susan and Ted were convinced his ratings would soar.

Jake politely declined to eat a sandwich with his dad and Susan. It was time to move on to the next phase of his campaign to win Sabrina. He drove to Jonah Merritt's house, where he found Sabrina's lime-green Beetle parked out front. She opened the front door to his knock.

"Are we going somewhere that I forgot about?" She glanced down at her hip-hugging jeans and fluoro-orange wrap T-shirt. She looked fantastic, as always.

"I came to tell you that I made things up with Dad," he said.

"I heard you on the radio."

And she hadn't called him. Jake deflated a little. He glanced beyond her, through the doorway. "Are you going to invite me in?"

"No."

"I came to tell you," he said, "that I love you."

She frowned. Definitely not the right reaction. His mouth dried up.

"I want us to get back together," he said. Dammit, this was hopeless, saying it on her doorstep. "Let me in, Sabrina. I want us to get engaged for real. Married."

"Why?"

He blinked. "I told you, I love you." He couldn't figure out what was going on, only that something was terribly wrong. His hands turned clammy. "So, will you?" he asked. "Marry me?"

To think people complimented him on his oratory skills.

Sabrina put one hand on the doorknob. "The radio report about your reconciliation with Ted," she said. "The station was flooded with calls from people saying they'll vote for you."

"So what?"

"They're predicting a win for you in the primary." Her voice shook.

A week ago, he'd have whooped for joy. "Sabrina, forget my dad, forget the election. I'm here to talk about us. I love you." Dammit, how many times did he need to say it?

She winced. "Jake, I'm glad you and Ted sorted things out. But it makes no difference to you and me. You've had more than a week to figure out you love me and want to marry me. But it's only now that it looks as if you'll be governor that you show up here. A governor needs a wife, and we both know I'm a damn good choice."

"That's stupid," he said.

She folded her arms and stared him down.

"Sabrina, I love you."

Something flared in her eyes, and he thought he'd gotten through. The she sighed. A letting-go sigh.

"I believe you care about me, Jake," she said. "But it's not enough."

She disappeared behind the door, and Jake found himself staring at solid wood. "What the hell happened here?" he wondered aloud.

He considered pounding on the door, breaking it down if necessary, and *making* Sabrina believe him.

But even if he could convince her today, if he won the election she would always harbor a nagging doubt that he loved her for herself. Beautiful and smart as she was, she lacked confidence.

Jake didn't want her ever to doubt him.

There was only one thing he could do.

He pulled out his cell phone and called Susan. As soon as she heard his voice, she burbled on about the support Jake was getting from the public, the upswing in his chances of winning. Jake let her hold on to the dream for a few more seconds.

"I need to call another press conference," he said. And he proceeded to ruin Susan's day so effectively that, in a burst of outrage, she quit.

CHAPTER FIFTEEN

SABRINA'S FATHER KNOCKED on her bedroom door at six the next morning, jerking her out of her beauty sleep in a way that couldn't be good for her. She'd had so little sleep since she left Jake, they'd be firing her from Miss Georgia for excess baggage. Under her eyes.

"Phone for you." Jonah held out the cordless. "A journalist." He looked at his watch and she gathered he'd only just refrained from threatening a harassment suit.

"Tell them to call back at nine," she said.

Her father sighed. "This is serious, Sabrina."

Serious? Had something happened to Jake? She grabbed the phone.

"This is Marlene Black's assistant from NewsBreak," a female voice said. "Marlene would like to invite you on to this morning's show to discuss your breakup with Jake Warrington."

It took a moment for what the woman had said to register. "Did you say, my *breakup* with Jake?" Reaching over to the night table, Sabrina switched on her cell phone.

"It's a chance to tell your side of the story," the woman said sympathetically.

What story, for Pete's sake? Sabrina's cell phone beeped to say she had thirty-two messages. Yikes. Obviously there was a story.

"Give me your number," Sabrina said. "I may call you back."

Her father was watching as she disconnected. "She said you and Jake broke up—is that true?"

"I, uh, I'm not sure." Sabrina pushed her hair back off her face. "Are there reporters outside?"

Her father went to the window, discreetly parted the curtains. "Dozens of them. All outside the gate." He sounded disappointed that he wouldn't get to have anyone arrested.

Sabrina groaned. "Dad, could you do me a favor and bring the newspaper in?"

Fifteen minutes later—her father refused to step outside without showering and dressing first—she was staring at the headline of the *Journal-Constitution*. Jake and Sabrina: It's Over.

"Why didn't you tell me?" her father demanded.

She waved him away and took a slug of her coffee.

Gubernatorial candidate Jake Warrington announced last night that his engagement to beauty queen Sabrina Merritt is over.

"Dammit, Jake," she muttered, "I got dumping rights." Could he have been so annoyed at her refusal to marry him that he'd decided to get in first?

Mr. Warrington declined to elaborate on the reasons for the split, but said he and Ms. Merritt remain friends.

"Only until I kill him," she said.

Ms. Merritt could not be reached for comment, but political commentators questioned the timing of the announcement, describing it as "foolhardy" and "a dangerous disruption for a candidate whose chances were always slim."

She groaned. "Couldn't you have waited just another day?"

The reporter had contacted as many of her and Jake's friends as he could, but had encountered nothing more than blank astonishment. Hardly surprising.

The article concluded:

Many voters expressed the opinion that Mr. Warrington is too "all over the place" to be a candidate for governor. Previous Warrington supporters are now declaring their intention to vote for other, more stable candidates.

Reading over her shoulder, Jonah said, "I don't understand the boy. Anyone would think he wants to lose tomorrow. He can't have thought through the consequences of this."

"Jake always thinks through the consequences."

Sabrina defended him automatically. Yet right now, it looked as if he hadn't....

After her father left the room, she called Jake. No answer. She knew for sure he wasn't worried about his beauty sleep, which meant he was ignoring her. She left him an acerbic message, ending with the instruction to "Call me. Now."

Jake had never been one to obey orders. She didn't hear from him all day, and she couldn't leave the house because of the crowd of reporters outside. She spent the day fending off her father's curiosity and refusing to take calls.

Inwardly, she worried about the demise of Jake's prospects in tomorrow's primary. Even if he'd broken her heart, she didn't want him to miss out on his life's dream. It was almost as if he'd forgotten what mattered most to him, she thought as she turned off the TV in her bedroom after the late news.

Or as if he's realized he was wrong.

Sabrina punched her pillow. "I'm an idiot," she told the empty room.

Jake's willingness to sacrifice the election, his reputation, could only mean one thing. He loved her!

He'd told her so, but she'd accused him of wanting a suitable wife. He was so determined to prove her wrong, stubborn fool, that he was making sure he didn't get elected.

"He loves me," she told her reflection in the mirror above the mantelpiece. She had to be right. Because if she was wrong, and she went ahead with the outrageous plan that had jumped into her head, she'd not only be humiliated, she'd be heartbroken a third time.

Sabrina went to her father's study to use the Internet. As she suspected, several local media organizations were running online polls, inviting Web visitors to say who they would vote for tomorrow. Jake sat at or near the bottom of every one.

Which meant the task ahead was enormous. Sabrina groaned. "I'll kill him," she said, "then I'll marry him."

Thankfully, while Jake's brain had been turning to mush, hers had been honed over the past few weeks to a fine, strategic weapon. She knew exactly what she had to do.

THE GUARANTEE OF AN exclusive on the hottest story of the week was enough to lure Marlene Black out of her studio and down to Sabrina's local polling station.

The TV crew filmed Sabrina going inside to vote. Afterward, Marlene interviewed her. It had started to rain, so, out of sight of the camera, a production assistant held an extra-large umbrella over them.

"Sabrina, who did you vote for?"

"I've been telling Georgians for the past few months that Jake Warrington is the best man for the job, Marlene, so naturally I voted for him." She gave her most scintillating smile.

"Even though he ended your engagement—" a pause "—without telling you?"

When Sabrina had given the woman that tidbit on the

phone, she'd just about fainted—and she hadn't yet heard the full story. The news reporters watching them started scribbling frantic notes.

"That made me mad," Sabrina admitted. "Particularly because he'd promised I could be the one to break it off."

Marlene's eyes sparkled. "Why would he make you a promise like that?"

"I have a confession." Sabrina had chosen the words because they were guaranteed to have every person in the state pause in chewing their cornflakes. "Our engagement was a fake—I forced Jake into it."

The camera wavered a second, and Marlene closed her eyes in a moment of journalistic ecstasy. Then she got down to business. "Tell me more."

So Sabrina did. She told the whole sorry story, starting with her chunky thighs and the loss of the job at the trust, through her fake engagement.

"Did Jake end the engagement because he wanted to come clean with the voters?" Marlene asked.

Sabrina hesitated. She didn't want to tell the world Jake was in love with her. She was hopeful, almost confident, but she wasn't an idiot. "I haven't talked to him yet, but it looks that way."

"How do you feel about Jake Warrington now?"

Sabrina couldn't stop the smile that spread over her face. "I love him, and I think he'll be the best governor this state has ever had. And the best husband a woman ever had. Jake's a real family man."

Some of the onlookers cheered. Marlene wasn't

done. "Sabrina, might I say before we finish here, that is a wonderful skirt."

Sabrina glanced down at the very micromini that showed a lot of her thighs. It was hardly a practical choice—the rain had turned to something nearer sleet—but Jake would love it. "Thank you," she said happily.

At last the interview was over. Marlene planned to return to her studio to air the segment right away—it would play within twenty minutes, she promised. Sabrina wanted to be with Jake when he watched it. She ran to her car, holding her purse over her head to protect her hair. She climbed behind the wheel of her VW Beetle— difficult to do decently in this skirt—and drove toward Jake's house.

She couldn't wait to see him. She sped up, and laughed as the car hit thirty miles an hour. Ha, she really was a new woman, a woman who could drive at the speed limit without fear. *I am woman, see me drive.*

As the rain grew heavier, she turned the wipers on faster. She couldn't remember what Susan had said about election day weather—if Jake's supporters were the kind who turned out rain or shine, or if this would deter them. As she reached Virginia Highlands—only another mile to Jake's place—her cell phone rang.

Jake, she'd bet. The reporters who'd been at the polling station would be after him already.

She was almost tempted to break her own don't-talk-and-drive rule. She glanced down at her phone on the passenger seat. Not Jake, her father.

She turned her attention back to the road.

Just in time to see the looming rear end of a carelessly parked truck.

The crash was a sickening cacophony of screeching, crunching, grinding metal. Sabrina flew forward in the fraction of a second before her seat belt locked, at the same time as the air bag inflated, slamming her back in her seat. She felt a burning heat, which she knew from past experience was the air bag.

The sequence was agonizingly familiar.

The noise, the smell of fuel, the shattered glass and the blaring of a horn assaulted Sabrina's senses. Images bombarded her—her mother's still, lifeless body, the blood, the desperate clawing at the door in an attempt to get out, the terrifying awareness that she couldn't feel her legs.

No, that was then. The other accident. Wasn't it?

Can I feel my legs? Pain and memory jumbled into a mishmash. Two accidents became one. Sobs wrenched from Sabrina's throat. She fumbled to unclip her seat belt, but failed. She didn't know what she could feel...if anything.

Every vestige of strength, of courage, of hard-won independence deserted her.

Sabrina screamed. And screamed. And screamed.

CHAPTER SIXTEEN

JAKE'S HEART LEAPED when he heard Sabrina talking to Marlene Black on the breakfast news. He looked up from his granola...then he saw the subtitle on the screen: Phony Engagement.

"What the—" He put down his bowl, dimly aware that every other person in the state would be doing the same thing right now, and turned up the volume.

As Sabrina continued talking, his jaw dropped. His crazy, beautiful, brilliant fiancée...couldn't she just let him do what he had to? Then Sabrina said, "I love him."

Jake whooped loud enough for the whole block to hear. "I love you, too, honey," he yelled at the screen, then looked around. He'd become one of those nutcases who talk to their TV sets. "Where are you?" he asked the television. "Come on home."

Damn, he'd switched off his cell phone and unplugged his landline to avoid the media. His answering machine flashed fifty-two messages. The cell phone rang the second he switched it on. It was Susan.

"I'm rescinding my resignation," she said.

"Later, Aunt Sue." He hung up on her. The phone

rang again, and this time he checked the display. Number withheld, probably his father. With a hiss of impatience, he took the call.

"Mr. Warrington, this is Emory University Hospital." The woman on the other end of the line lowered her voice. "I shouldn't be calling you because you're not next of kin…but you should know Sabrina Merritt was just brought in here following a traffic accident."

The floor tipped beneath his feet—he grasped the back of the couch. "Is she…okay?"

She wasn't, he knew it.

The rushing sound in Jake's ears almost prevented him from hearing the woman, who was talking even more quietly.

"She's unconscious…they're doing tests. We'll know more in the next hour. Do you want me to—"

"I'm coming," Jake croaked.

JAKE ARRIVED AT THE hospital at the same time as Sabrina's father. The normally ebullient Jonah tottered across the parking lot like an old man on his last legs. He raised a limp hand in greeting, his eyes fixed on the building in front of them.

"How much have you heard?" Jake asked.

Jonah shook his head. "Next to nothing."

Jake had prayed all the way here. Now, he prayed again, begging God to let Sabrina be okay. Let her spine be unharmed.

Inside, they were shown to a waiting room and told that a doctor would see them as soon as possible.

Cynthia and Megan arrived a few minutes later, followed by Ted and Susan, Tyler and Bethany. No one said much beyond their initial greeting—they all knew how bad this could be. Jake looked around the room at all these people who loved Sabrina. *I love her more, and I never showed her.* His eyes felt hot, his chin like Jell-O.

"She can't go through this again," Jonah said into the silence. He started to pace, but almost immediately lost strength and leaned one hand on the pale peach wall. "Learning to walk, those months in bed...she can't do it."

"It'll kill her," Megan said, her face pale. "Poor Baby."

Susan sobbed quietly; Ted put an arm around her, pulled her close. Which drew a few curious glances.

"She'll get through it." Jake's volume surprised him, as well as everyone else. Heads turned toward him.

"Sabrina can do anything she sets her mind to," he said. "And then some. She's the strongest person I know."

"She's suffered so much," Cynthia began, her brow furrowed.

"And she's tougher for it." Jake glanced out into the corridor, at a passing trolley loaded with floral deliveries for patients, and willed Sabrina to be fighting back, right now. "You all look at her and see the girl who almost broke. I'm telling you to look again."

He sounded as if he was campaigning...and he was. He was campaigning for the most important victory of his life. "Look again, see a woman who lost her mother, lost her ability to walk, almost lost her life, but still came back. I know she let you pamper her, and she made the most of it—" he found himself grinning at the thought of Sabrina's feigned tears "—but if you can't see she's more than capable of beating whatever this accident has dealt her, then she's smarter than all of you."

Jonah's expression darkened, but Jake continued, "You have a daughter to be proud of, Jonah. Not for her beauty, but for her brains, her courage, her persistence."

"I am proud of her," Jonah growled, but he sounded uncertain. Then his voice cracked. "I love her. If I lose her, I don't know what I'll…" He shuddered convulsively.

Megan put an arm around his shoulders. "We know, Dad. Sabrina's special." She seemed about to burst into tears.

"Just because Sabrina's special, that doesn't mean she needs to be treated with kid gloves," Jake persisted.

"You're an expert on how to treat my daughter, are you?" Jonah demanded. He sank into gloom again. "If she pulls through this, I'm going to take such good care of her."

"No, you won't," Jake said.

Jonah's face reddened.

"Hell, Jonah, I understand what you're saying." Jake paced across the room and back. "I feel the same myself, like I want to take her home and never let her out. But she'll never forgive you if you try and coddle her, and she'll never forgive me, either." He thought about the way she'd put Megan in her place at dinner the other week. "You're a braver man than I am if you'll risk her anger."

"I'm her father," Jonah said.

"And I'm the man she's going to marry."

Cynthia put a hand to her mouth. "Oh, no, I haven't voted yet."

Jake had forgotten all about the primary. "Doesn't matter."

"I'm going to find a doctor, and they're damn well going to let me see my daughter." Jonah flung himself out of the room.

Jake followed, intercepting the older man in the hallway.

"Jonah." Jake put a hand on his arm. Jonah tried to shake it off.

"Don't you dare go in there and scare Sabrina with your fears." Jake's voice was low and controlled, but sufficiently menacing to check Jonah's progress.

"Don't you tell me—" he sputtered.

"If you do," Jake said deliberately, "I will tell her about your attempts to influence the judges of the Miss Georgia Pageant."

Jonah paled. "I didn't—"

"You did," Jake said. "She's so proud of that win, but thanks to you, we'll never know if she would have made it on her own strengths."

"Of course she…" Jonah trailed off, realizing it was miserably clear he hadn't believed his daughter would win. "I just wanted—"

"To protect her," Jake said. "Jonah, I love your daughter, I'm going to marry her. From now on, if there's any protecting to be done, it's my job. But I can tell you, it's one I'll take up reluctantly, and only ever with Sabrina's permission."

Jonah stared at Jake for a long time. Hospital personnel bustled past, jostling them. At last, he inclined his head. "I won't upset her. It's the last thing I want."

He allowed Jake to shepherd him back into the room.

"Did you see her?" Megan asked.

"I decided to wait for the doctor," Jonah announced grudgingly.

When the door opened, they all looked up. Jake tried not to feel disappointed when Max walked in. "I was at one of our sites," he said. "I only just got your message, Mom."

Susan hugged him. "There's no news yet." She stepped back, but held on to Max's hands. Tears sprang to her eyes.

"Mom?" Max said, alarmed.

Susan gripped tighter. "I've been thinking how dreadful it would be if you were in an accident and ended up dying unhappy."

"Hard to be happy about dying in an accident," Max observed uncomfortably.

Jake snorted. Susan swatted Max's arm. "That's not what I mean. You're such a wonderful son, a wonderful businessman, but you haven't found a woman to love."

"Mom…" Max got a hunted look; he glanced toward the exit.

"I'm not just talking about you. We all need to find the person who's going to make us happy and seize the chance for love with both hands." Susan shook his shoulders. "That's what I'm going to do."

"Go for it, Mom." Max managed to free himself from her grasp.

"As a matter of fact, I will." Susan twirled on her heel, almost girlish. "Ted, there's something I want to say."

Jake's father gave her a slow, intimate smile. As if he knew what was coming. Jake didn't have a clue.

"If, as Jake says, we can expect Sabrina to recover from this accident no matter how bad it is," Susan said, "then I think I need to expect more of myself."

Ted started to laugh. "My love, if you're likening being with me to being in a car wreck…"

My love? Was something going on between Ted and Susan? Jake felt as if he'd missed the bus and was running along behind it.

"I'm doing no such thing." Susan wagged a finger at him. "I'm talking about trusting you."

"A marvelous idea," Ted said.

"Then somehow, we're going to have to make it work, if you still want it to. I have no idea how—I mean, where will we live? One of us is going to have to sacrifice a lot." She drew a breath. "But some things are worth sacrificing for."

"Mom, what are you talking about?" Max grabbed her wrist.

Susan tugged free. "I'm talking about love and forgiveness and being willing to start over." She swung back to Ted. "Ted, I'm sorry I hurt you. I've missed you these past few days, I've missed everything about you. If you still think there's anything between us, I hope you'll give it a chance to…to blossom," she ended uncertainly, as if she'd only just realized how exposed she was, declaring herself in front of everyone.

Ted's grin was wide enough for two men. "Susan, dearest, you're the woman for me, and that's not going to change. Whatever you have to give up for me, I'll give double for you."

She stepped into his arms, blushing like a sixteen-year-old. "Really?"

"Take my heart," he murmured. "My life." Then he kissed her, right there in the waiting room.

"You don't mind, boys, do you?" Susan asked belatedly when Ted released her.

Tyler had levered himself out of his chair the moment Ted started kissing Susan. Jake figured the only reason his cousin hadn't punched Ted was because, like Jake, he was still trying to absorb the news.

"It's great, isn't it?" Jake made his own decision as he prompted Tyler.

"Uh, yeah." Tyler's fingers moved at his side, loosened. "Yeah, Mom, it really is great."

"Just so long as we don't have to watch anything like that again," Max muttered.

Susan laughed and embraced her sons; Ted shook their hands.

Jonah and his daughters added their congratulations, but Jonah seemed distracted. "How long can it take?" he muttered, with yet another glance at the door.

His question was answered a few minutes later, when a doctor walked in. "Family of Sabrina Merritt?"

Jonah jumped to his feet. "I'm her father."

Jake was right beside him. "I'm her fiancé."

"Ah—" the doctor gave a small smile "—you must be *that idiot, Jake Warrington.*"

"That's me," Jake said proudly. "She's awake, right?"

"Very much so," the doctor said. He turned to Jonah, "She has some bruising, but no serious injury."

Jonah gave a cry of relief.

"She's up to receiving one visitor."

As Jonah made for the door, the doctor detained him. "Mr. Merritt, your daughter has stated in no uncertain terms that Jake Warrington is to be that visitor."

At least she'd known he'd be here, Jake thought. He hadn't totally destroyed her faith in him.

He followed the doctor down the hallway. On the way, they passed another florist's trolley. Jake had been in such a hurry to get here, it hadn't occurred to him to bring flowers. He didn't hesitate; he twisted a pale mauve orchid off its stem. As they reached Sabrina's room, he steeled himself for the sight of the medical equipment and of her looking awful—as awful as Sabrina could—so he wouldn't be tempted to do anything stupid, like forbid her ever to go anywhere without him again.

But the moment he saw her, porcelain pale, her wrists thin where they rested on the coverlet, red burns on her nose and forehead from the air bag, his resolution failed. All he wanted was to gather her into his arms and hold on to her for the rest of his life.

Her eyes met his, and filled with tears, worsening the temptation.

"I'm a wimp," she said.

"Huh? Sweetheart, what do you mean?"

She gripped the coverlet. "Jake, I keep telling you how strong I am, how independent. But when I crashed my car today—" she gulped "—I screamed my head off. I couldn't stop. I was terrified." She turned her head aside, and Jake saw a tear on her cheek.

She needed more from him than his undying commitment to look after her. She needed to know she was strong.

He prized her fingers off the blanket and nestled the orchid he'd filched into her palm. "Sabrina," he said, "you are about the bravest woman in the world. I don't know anyone who wouldn't have screamed at what happened to you today, including me."

She smiled sheepishly. "You would not."

"Like a girl," he vowed. "Honey, I don't ever want to let you behind the wheel of a car again—" she opened her mouth, and he held up his hand "—but the day you get out of hospital, if the doctor says you're able, you're going to drive."

She blanched.

"Because you'll want to do it," he said. "And I know you can do whatever you want."

She lifted her chin, looked him in the eye. "What if I want to marry you?" Her voice held the faintest quaver.

"Hell, yes, you can do that." Jake couldn't contain his grin, then his laugh. "In fact, I insist." He kissed her, mindful of her injuries, with a tender passion that caught him off guard.

"I love you," he said when he released her.

Sabrina smirked. "I know."

"Of course you do, you're smart." He kissed her again.

"I love you, too." That called for another kiss. "Thanks for the flower." She held up the orchid, now slightly crushed. "Could you only afford one?"

He laughed. "It's like you, sweetheart. Unique."

Her eyes misted over.

There was a commotion in the hallway outside, cheering, scuffling, and then they heard a nurse say, "Absolutely not, you can't go in there."

Next moment, Ted stuck his head around the door. "The exit polls are unanimous, so much so they're already predicting the result." He did a little jig in the doorway. "Seems the voters like a man whose woman stands by him. You're going to win the primary, Jake. Next stop, the governor's mansion."

Sabrina caught her breath. "Jake, you did it." The tears that had been flowing readily since this morning's accident made a fresh appearance.

Jake pulled out a handkerchief, wiped her cheeks. Which made her cry harder. She loved that he respected her independence, but she cherished this tenderness, knowing that it was just for her, because he loved her.

"Your face is going red," he said helpfully, reminding her she hadn't seen a mirror since this morning.

She touched the burn on her nose. "I must look awful."

"Hideous," he said. "But I still love you."

"You just keep telling it like it is," she said. "Don't spare my feelings."

He caressed her cheek. "Okay, here's how it is." He took her hands. "Sabrina, I love you so much, I can't wait to marry you. You mean more to me than anything else, and you always will."

She got a lump in her throat the size of a baseball. "That's all very well for you," she said. "But you know I'm not good at sticking with things. What if I change my mind?"

"Brat." He flicked her chin. "I won't let you. Besides, you've been in love with me five years already—I think that shows excellent stickability."

"Jerk."

Jake grinned. "I see we're on track for some peace in the home," he murmured against her lips.

* * * * *

Don't miss the second book of
THOSE MERRITT GIRLS.
Look for HER SECRET RIVAL
by Abby Gaines in November 2009
from Harlequin Superromance.

Silhouette®

Romantic
SUSPENSE

Sparked by Danger, Fueled by Passion.

The Agent's Secret Baby

by *USA TODAY* bestselling author
Marie Ferrarella

TOP SECRET DELIVERIES

Dr. Eve Walters suddenly finds herself pregnant
after a regrettable one-night stand and turns to an
online chat room for support. She eventually learns
the true identity of her one-night stand: a DEA agent
with a deadly secret. Adam Serrano does not want
this baby or a relationship, but can fear for Eve's
and the baby's lives convince him that this is what
he has been searching for after all?

Available October wherever books are sold.

**Look for upcoming titles in
the TOP SECRET DELIVERIES miniseries**
The Cowboy's Secret Twins by Carla Cassidy—November
The Soldier's Secret Daughter by Cindy Dees—December

Visit Silhouette Books at www.eHarlequin.com

REQUEST YOUR FREE BOOKS!

2 FREE NOVELS PLUS 2 FREE GIFTS!

HARLEQUIN®

Super Romance®

Exciting, emotional, unexpected!

YES! Please send me 2 FREE Harlequin® Superromance® novels and my 2 FREE gifts (gifts are worth about $10). After receiving them, if I don't wish to receive any more books, I can return the shipping statement marked "cancel." If I don't cancel, I will receive 6 brand-new novels every month and be billed just $4.69 per book in the U.S. or $5.24 per book in Canada. That's a savings of close to 15% off the cover price! It's quite a bargain! Shipping and handling is just 50¢ per book*. I understand that accepting the 2 free books and gifts places me under no obligation to buy anything. I can always return a shipment and cancel at any time. Even if I never buy another book from Harlequin, the two free books and gifts are mine to keep forever.

135 HDN EYLG   336 HDN EYLS

Name	(PLEASE PRINT)	
Address		Apt. #
City	State/Prov.	Zip/Postal Code

Signature (if under 18, a parent or guardian must sign)

Mail to the **Harlequin Reader Service:**
IN U.S.A.: P.O. Box 1867, Buffalo, NY 14240-1867
IN CANADA: P.O. Box 609, Fort Erie, Ontario L2A 5X3

Not valid to current subscribers of Harlequin Superromance books.

**Are you a current subscriber of Harlequin Superromance books
and want to receive the larger-print edition?
Call 1-800-873-8635 today!**

* Terms and prices subject to change without notice. Prices do not include applicable taxes. Sales tax applicable in N.Y. Canadian residents will be charged applicable provincial taxes and GST. Offer not valid in Quebec. This offer is limited to one order per household. All orders subject to approval. Credit or debit balances in a customer's account(s) may be offset by any other outstanding balance owed by or to the customer. Please allow 4 to 6 weeks for delivery. Offer available while quantities last.

Your Privacy: Harlequin is committed to protecting your privacy. Our Privacy Policy is available online at www.eHarlequin.com or upon request from the Reader Service. From time to time we make our lists of customers available to reputable third parties who may have a product or service of interest to you. If you would prefer we not share your name and address, please check here. ☐

HSR09R

In 2009 Harlequin celebrates
60 years of pure reading pleasure!

We're marking this occasion by offering
16 **FREE** full books to download and read.

Visit

www.HarlequinCelebrates.com

to choose from a variety of
great romance stories
that are absolutely **FREE!**

(Total approximate retail value of $60)

We invite you to visit and share the Web site
with your friends, family
and anyone who enjoys reading.

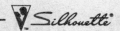

SPECIAL EDITION

FROM *NEW YORK TIMES* BESTSELLING AUTHOR

SUSAN MALLERY

DESERT ROGUES

THE SHEIK AND THE BOUGHT BRIDE

Victoria McCallan works in Prince Kateb's palace. When Victoria's gambling father is caught cheating at cards with the prince, Victoria saves her father from going to jail by being Kateb's mistress for six months. But the darkly handsome desert sheik isn't as harsh as Victoria thinks he is, and Kateb finds himself attracted to his new mistress. But Kateb has already loved and lost once—is he willing to give love another try?

Available in October wherever books are sold.

SSE65481

HARLEQUIN *Super Romance*

COMING NEXT MONTH

Available October 13, 2009

#1590 FOR THE LOVE OF FAMILY • Kathleen O'Brien
The Diamond Legacy
Every family has secrets, but Belle Carson has an old one that's a doozy! Entangled with newfound relatives, Belle finds things getting more complicated when she starts falling for her new boss, Matt Malone. And now she's keeping a few secrets from him Don't you just hate it when history repeats itself?

#1591 HIS SECRET AGENDA • Beth Andrews
Dean can't fall for Allie Martin—he's working her! And when the ex-lawyer finds out that Dean Garret's not the laid-back cowboy bartender she hired, their passion could turn from love to hate as fast as it takes him to whip up a margarita....

#1592 MADISON'S CHILDREN • Linda Warren
The Belles of Texas
Madison Belle can't have children and is resigned to the single life. Until she meets Walker, the law of High Cotton, Texas, and his two adorable kids. She's falling in love and life is perfect, until his ex-wife shows up...carrying his child.

#1593 HER BEST BET • Pamela Ford
When Izzy Gordon's friend bets her there's no way she'll marry her oh-so-perfect boyfriend, Izzy thinks it's money in the bank. Then she meets Gib Murphy, and Izzy can't stop thinking about him. Maybe the smarter money is on Gib!

#1594 NEXT COMES LOVE • Helen Brenna
An Island to Remember
From the moment Erica Corelli steps off the ferry with a little boy in tow, Sheriff Garrett Taylor's plans for a quiet life are jeopardized. And it's not just the trouble following her. Garrett can't seem to fight the attraction igniting between them.

#1595 THE MAN SHE ONCE KNEW • Jean Brashear
Going Back
Callie Hunter would give anything not to be back in this town. Still, she has a duty to do, so here she is. Not much has changed...except for David Langley—the first boy sh loved. This David bears little resemblance to the one she knew, but it seems her heart doesn't recognize the difference.

HSRCNMBPA0909